George Manville Fenn

A Double Knot

A novel. Vol. 1

George Manville Fenn

A Double Knot
A novel. Vol. 1

ISBN/EAN: 9783337065928

Printed in Europe, USA, Canada, Australia, Japan

Cover: Foto ©Andreas Hilbeck / pixelio.de

More available books at **www.hansebooks.com**

A DOUBLE KNOT

A Novel

BY

GEORGE MANVILLE FENN

AUTHOR OF

'ELI'S CHILDREN,' 'THE MASTER OF THE CEREMONIES,' ETC., ETC.

IN THREE VOLUMES

VOL. I.

London

METHUEN & CO.

18, BURY STREET, BLOOMSBURY, W.C.

1890

CONTENTS OF VOL. I.

—◦—

PROLOGUE.—THE GERM.

THE STORY.—YEARS AGO.

A DOUBLE KNOT.

PROLOGUE.—THE GERM.

CHAPTER I.

A DAUGHTER OF EVE.

'MOTHER!'

There was no reply, and once again rose from the bed in the prettily-furnished room the same word— 'Mother!' The wild, appealing, anguished cry of offspring to parent, seeming to ask for help—protec- tion—forgiveness—the tenderness of the mother- heart to its young, and still there was no answer.

The speaker struggled up so that she rested on her elbow, the heavy dark nut-brown hair fell in long clusters on her soft white neck and bosom; her large hazel eyes looked wild and dilated; and her fair young face deathly pale, as, with quivering white lips, she cried once more:

'Mother! Speak to me or I shall die.'

'It would be better so,' was the cold hard reply, and a lady who had been gazing from the window turned slowly round to gaze full at the first speaker, her handsome Spanish type of countenance looking malignant as her dark eyes flashed, where she stood biting her full sensuous nether lip, and glaring at the occupant of the bed.

'Mother!' was the anguished cry once more, as the girl sank back upon her pillow.

'Yes,' was the bitter reply. 'You are a mother. God be thanked that your father, who idolized his child, was not spared to see this day.'

'Oh, mother, mother, have some pity—have some mercy upon me. Where am I to seek it, if not from you?'

'From Heaven: for the world will show you none. Why should I? Shame upon you that you should bring this curse upon my widowed life. The coward!—the villain! Was not our simple quiet home, far away from the busy world, to be held sacred, that he must seek us out and cast such a blight upon it !'

'Oh, hush, mother !' wailed the girl. 'I love him—I love him.'

'Love him ! Idiot ! Baby ! To be led away by the smooth words of the first soft-spoken villain you meet.'

'You shall not call him villain, mamma,' cried the girl passionately. 'He loves me, and I am to be his wife.'

The girl flashed up for a moment with anger, but only to lie back the next instant faint and with half-closed eyes.

'His wife ! Are you such a fool that you believe this?' cried the elder woman bitterly. 'His wife ! There, cast aside that shadow at once, for it is a delusion.'

'No, no, mother, dear mother, he has promised me that I shall be his wife, and I believe him.'

'Yes,' said the mother, 'as thousands of daughters of Eve have believed before. There, cast away that thought, poor fool, and think now of hiding your sin from the world which will shun you as if you had the plague.'

'Mother!' cried the girl piteously.

'Don't talk to me!' cried the woman fiercely, and she began to pace the room; tall, swarthy, and handsome for her years, her mobile countenance betraying the workings of the passionate spirit within her.

'Mother! Would I had never been one! My life has been a curse to me.'

'No, no; don't say that, dear.'

'It has, I tell you. There's something wrong in our blood, I suppose. Look at your brother.'

'Poor Julian!' sighed the girl.

'Poor Julian!' cried the woman scornfully. 'Of course he is poor, and he deserves it. He must have been mad.'

'But he loved her, mamma, so dearly.'

'Loved!' cried the woman with a wild intensity of rage in her deep rich voice and gesture, as she spat on the floor. 'Curse love! Curse it! What has it done for me? A few sickly embraces—a few years of what the world calls happiness—and then a widowhood of poverty and misery.'

'Mamma, you will kill me if you talk like that.'

'Then I will talk like that, and save myself from temptation more than I can bear,' cried the woman fiercely. 'What has love done for the son of whom I was so proud—my gallant-looking, handsome boy? Why, with his bold, noble, Spanish face and dark eyes, he might have wed some heiress, married whom he liked—and what does he do? turns himself into a galley slave.'

'Mamma, what are you saying?' cried the girl faintly.

'The truth. What has he done? Married a woman without a *sou*, and had to accept that post at the mines. Isn't that being a galley slave?'

'But he loved Delia, mamma.'

'Loved her! Curse love! I tell you. The ass! The idiot, to be led away by that sickly, washed-out creature—the Honourable Delia Dymcox,' she continued, with an intensity of scorn in her tones.

'But she is a lady, mamma.'

'Lady? The family are paupers, and, forsooth,

they must look down on him—on us because we have
no blood.   Well, she is justly punished, and he too.
I hope they like Auvergne.'

'Oh, mother,' sighed the girl weakly, 'you are very
cruel.'

'Cruel?   I wish I had been cruel enough to
have strangled you both at birth.   I wish our
family were at an end—that it would die out as
Julian's brats waste away there in that hot, dry, sun-
cursed region.'

'You do not mean it, dear?'

'I do, Mary; I swear I do.   Oh that I could have
been so weak as to marry as I did—to be cursed with
two such children !'

'You talk so, dear, because you are angry with
me,' sighed the girl.   'I know you loved poor papa
dearly.'

'Pish !   You are like him.'

'Yes, mamma, and poor Julian has always been so
like you.'

There was silence then in the half-shadowed
room, while the mother sat sternly gazing out at the
stream that rippled by the cottage, dancing in the sun-

light and bathing the roots of the willows that kissed
its dimpling, silvery surface. The verdant meadows
stretched far away rich in the lush grass and many
flowers that dotted them with touches of light. All
without looked bright and joyous, as a lark high
poised poured forth his lay, which seemed to vibrate
in the blue arch of heaven, and then fall in silvery
fragments slowly down to earth.

The girl lay crying silently, the tears moistening
her soft white pillow, as she gazed piteously from
time to time at her mother's averted face, half
hidden from her by the white curtain she held aside
to gaze from the window.

'Can you—can you see him coming, mamma?'
faltered the girl at last.

'Whom? The doctor?' was the cold response,
as the curtain was allowed to fall back in its place.
'No, I have not sent for one. Why should we
publish our shame?'

'Our shame, mamma?'

'Yes, our shame. Is it not as bitter for me?
Live or die, I shall send for no doctor here.' Again
there was silence, and the elder woman slowly paced

the room, till, passing near the bed, a soft white
arm stole forth, and caught her hand.

'You are very cruel to me, mother. Oh, do
look; look again. See if he is coming.'

'If he is coming!' cried the elder. 'Are you mad
as well as weak? You will never see him more.
Poor fool! I believe even his name is only assumed.'

'I shall,' cried the girl with energy, 'and he will
come. He loves me too dearly to forsake me now.
He is a gentleman and the soul of honour.'

Her face lit up, and the joyous look of love shone
in her eyes as she gazed defiantly at her mother,
who looked back at her, half pitying, half mocking
her faith. Then, in spite of herself, she started, for
steps were heard on the path beneath, and as the
girl struggled up once more to her elbow, and
craned her neck towards the window, voices were
heard speaking at a little distance.

'There, there,' cried the girl, with a sob of joy, as
she sank back laughing hysterically. 'What did I
say? He loves me—he loves me, and he has come.'

Mrs. Riversley ran to the window, and drew aside
the curtain furtively as a couple of young men,

gentlemen evidently, and one carrying a trout rod, walked slowly by, following the winding path that led round by the great gravel pit in the wood that bordered the stream, and soon after they disappeared amidst the trees.

'That was his step,' cried the girl at last. 'Who was with him, mamma?'

'Captain Millet.'

'Poor Mr. Millet!' said the girl softly; and then, with the anxious troubled look fading from her countenance to give place to one of quiet content as a smile played round her lips, she lay very still, with half-closed eyes listening for the returning steps.

Twice she started up to listen, but only to sink back again, very calm and patient, her full faith that the man she loved would return beaming from every feature of her handsome young face.

'Mother,' she said at last softly; and Mrs. Riversley turned towards her.

'What do you want?'

'Is it not time you brought it back to me, mother —that you laid it by my side?'

There was no reply, and the girl looked up pleadingly.

'I should like him to see it when he comes,' she said softly, and a wondrous look of love dawned in her pale face, causing a strange pang in her mother's breast as she stood watching her and evidently trying to nerve herself for the disclosure she was about to make, one which in her anger she had thought easy, but which now became terribly difficult.

'If you cannot forgive me, mother dear,' said the girl pleadingly, 'let me have my babe : for I love it, I love it,' she whispered to herself, and the soft dawn of a young mother's yearning for her offspring grew warmer in her face.

'You will never see it more,' exclaimed the woman at last, in a hard harsh voice, though she trembled and shrank from her daughter's eyes as she spoke. 'It will never lie by your side for him to gaze upon your shame and his : the child is dead.'

A piteous cry broke from the young mother's breast, and in her bitter grief she lay sobbing violently, till nature interposed, and, exhausted, weak and helpless, she sank into a heavy sleep with the tears still wet upon her face.

'It is better so—it is better so,' muttered Mrs. Riversley, as she stood gazing down at her child. 'It will nearly kill her, but, God forgive me, it must be done.'

She stood watching in the shaded room till a slight noise below made her start, and hastily glancing at her daughter to see that she slept, she stole on tiptoe from the bedside, and crept downstairs to where a sharp angular-looking woman of four or five and twenty was standing in the little drawing-room with her shawl over one arm, and her bonnet swinging from the strings.

She looked flushed with exercise, and her hair about her temples was wet with perspiration, while her boots were covered with dust.

'Well?'

'Well,' said the woman, with a rude, impatient gesture. 'You must give me a glass of wine. I'm dead beat. It's quite four miles there, and as hot as hot.'

'How dare you speak to me in that insolent way, Jane!' said Mrs. Riversley angrily.

' Oh,' said the woman sharply, ' this is no time
far ma'aming and bowing and scraping; servants
and missuses is all human beings together when
they're in trouble, and folks don't make no difference
between them.'

' But you might speak in a more respectful way,
Jane,' said Mrs. Riversley, biting her lips, and looking
pale.

' Dessay I might,' said the woman ; ' but this ain't
the time.   Well, you want to know about the——'

' Hush ! for Heaven's sake, hush,' exclaimed Mrs.
Riversley, glancing round.

' Oh, there's no one near us,' said the woman with
a mocking laugh; ' not even the police, so you
needn't be afraid.   It ain't murder.'

' Did you find her ?' said Mrs. Riversley.   ' Pray
tell me, Jane.   I spoke rather harshly just now,
but I could not help it, I was so troubled and
upset.'

' Dessay you were ; dessay everybody else is,' said
the woman roughly.   ' How's Miss Mary ?'

' Better, Jane; but you must never see her again.
She must never know.'

' Did you tell her it was dead ?' said the woman sharply.

' Yes, yes, and so it must be to her. But tell me,' continued Mrs. Riversley eagerly, 'did you make the arrangement ?'

'Yes, and I had to give her every penny of the money you started me with.'

' And she does not know anything ?'

' No,' said the woman, 'and never will if you behave to me proper.'

' Yes, yes, Jane, I will ; anything I can do, but you must go from here—at once.'

' And how are you going to manage ?'

' As I can,' said Mrs. Riversley sternly. ' This secret must be kept.'

' And what are you going to give me to keep it ?' said the woman sharply.

' I am not rich, Jane—far from it,' began Mrs. Riversley.

' You're rich enough to pay me twenty pounds a year always,' said the woman, with a keen greedy look in her unpleasant face.

' Yes, yes, Jane, I will,' said Mrs. Riversley eagerly,

'on condition that you keep it secret, and never come near us more.'

'Then I want that gray silk dress of Miss Mary's,' said the woman, with the avaricious look growing in her face. 'She won't want to wear it now.'

'You shall have it, Jane.'

'And there's that velvet jacket I should like.'

'You shall have that too, Jane.'

'I ain't got a watch and chain,' said the woman, 'you may as well give me yourn.'

Without a word Mrs. Riversley unhooked the little gold watch from her side, drew the chain from her neck, and threw it over that of her servant, whose closely set eyes twinkled with delight.

'You must pay me the money in advance every year,' said the woman now sharply. 'I'm not going without the first year.'

Without replying Mrs. Riversley walked to a side table, unlocked a desk, and from the drawer took out four crisp new bank-notes.

Jane Glyne, maid-of-all-work at the Dingle, a place two miles from everywhere, as she said, and at which she was sure no decent servant would stop, held out her crooked fingers for the money, but Mrs. Riversley placed the hand containing the notes behind her.

'One word first,' she said firmly. 'I have agreed in every respect to the hard terms you have made.'

'Well, if you call them hard terms ——' began the woman in an insolent tone.

'Silence!' exclaimed Mrs. Riversley, 'and listen to me.'

She spoke in a low deep voice, full of emotion, and the low-bred woman quailed before her as she went on.

'I say I have come to your terms that you have imposed upon me.'

'I never imposed upon you,' began Jane.

'Silence, woman!' cried Mrs. Riversley, stamping her foot imperiously. 'I have agreed to all you wished, but I must have my conditions too. You have that unfortunate babe.'

'Your grandson,' said the woman in a low voice, but Mrs. Riversley did not heed her.

'Bring it up as you will, or trust it to whom you

will, but from this hour it must be dead to us. I shall give you the money in my hand, and I will do more. This is June. From now every half year fifteen pounds shall be ready at an address in London that I will give you. To such a woman as you that should be a goodly sum, but my conditions are that within an hour you shall have made up a bundle of the best of your things, and left this place, never to return. If you ever molest us by letter or visit, the money will be stopped.'

'And suppose I tell everybody about it ?' said the woman insolently.

'It is no criminal proceeding that I am aware of,' said Mrs. Riversley coldly; 'but you will not do that; you value the money too much. Do you agree to my terms ?'

'But my box,' said the woman. 'I can't carry away half my things.'

'Here is another five-pound note,' said Mrs. Riversley coldly ; 'five five-pound notes. I gave you ten pounds before, and you only gave that woman half.'

'How do you know ?'

'Because I know your grasping character,' said Mrs. Riversley firmly. 'Now—quick—do you decide? Try to extort more, and finding what you are, I shall risk all discovery, and bear the shame sooner than be under your heel.   Do you agree?'

'Yes,' said the woman surlily.

'Quick, then; get your things and go.   I will bring you the dress and jacket.'

'Ain't I to say good-bye to Miss Mary?'

'No,' said Mrs. Riversley firmly.   'Now go.'

The woman stood biting the side of one of her fingers for a few moments, and seemed to hesitate; but the rustle of the new bank-notes as Mrs. Riversley laid them upon the table and placed a paper-weight upon them decided her, and in an incredibly short time she stood once more in the room, in her best clothes, and with a bulky bundle tied up in an old Paisley shawl.

Five minutes later she had received the money without a word being spoken on either side, and was standing just out of sight of the cottage, by the stream, hugging the bundle to her with one hand, and gnawing at the side of her finger.

'What a fool I was!' she muttered viciously.
'She'd have given double if I'd pressed her, and I'm
put off now with a beggarly thirty pound a year. I've
a good mind to go back.'

She took a few steps in the direction of the cottage,
but stopped with a grim chuckle.

'Thirty pound a year regular for doing nothing is
better than ten pound and lots of work. Perhaps
we should only quarrel, for she's a hard one when
she's up. But I might have had more.'

She stood thinking for a few moments.

'What shall I do?' she muttered. 'If I leave it
with them they'll kill it in a week, and then there's
an end of it, and I get my money for nothing. If I
fetch it away I have to keep it. But it may be worth
my while. Mrs. Riversley ain't everybody, for there's
Miss Mary, and there's him, and if he isn't a swell,
t'other one is, I'm sure. What's that?'

She started in affright, for just then a strange,
hoarse shriek rang out of the wood to her left, and
it sounded so wild and agonizing that she stood
trembling and listening for awhile.

'It was like as if someone had jumped into one of

the deep river holes or the big pit,' she muttered ; ' but I dursen't go to see.   It was very horrid.'

Whatever the cry, it was not repeated, and the woman hurried on for about a mile, when, coming to a side lane, she hesitated as to the course she should take, and ended by going straight on.

At the end of a score of paces she stopped short, turned and hurried back to the side lane, down which she walked as fast as her bundle would let her.

' I don't care, I will,' she muttered ; ' thirty pound a year will keep us both.   I'll fetch him away; he may be worth his weight in gold.'

CHAPTER II.

THEY were about equal in height and build, and apparently within a year of the same age, the one dark, and wearing, what was unusual in those days, a short crisp beard and moustache; the other fair and closely shaven as to lip and chin, but with a full brown whisker clothing his cheeks.

The former was evidently terribly agitated, for his face worked and he was very pallid, while the latter looked flushed and nervous, the hand that grasped his trout-rod twitching convulsively; and he kept glancing at his companion as they strode along past the cottage.

'What I ask you is——' the darker of the two was saying.

'For Heaven's sake be silent till we get farther on, Rob, and I'll tell you all you want to know.'

There was silence for awhile, and the two young men walked rapidly on, turning through a woodland path, when the trees caught the rod of the one addressed as Rob, and he cast it impatiently aside, stopping short directly after in an opening where the path wound round the brink of a deep gravel-pit, the wayfarer being protected from a fall by a stout oaken railing.

'Now, sir,' exclaimed the first speaker excitedly; 'no one can hear us.'

'No,' said the fair man in a nervous, hesitating way. 'Go on; say what you have to say.'

'It is soon said, James Huish. I have been away with my regiment in Canada two years. Previous to that chance threw me into the company of a sweet, pure girl, little more than a child then. I used to come down here fishing.'

'You did!' exclaimed the other hoarsely.

'I did, and visited at that cottage time after time. Man, man, I tell you,' he continued, speaking rapidly in his excitement, 'the recollection of those days has been my solace in many a bitter winter's night, and I have looked forward to my return as the great day of my existence.'

'Stop!' said the other nervously. 'Tell me this, Rob: did she—did she love you?'

'Love me?' exclaimed the other passionately: 'no. How could I expect it? She was a mere child, budding into maidenhood; but her eyes brightened when I came, and she was my little companion here in the happy days that can never be recalled. James Huish, I loved that girl with all my soul. My love has grown for her, and my first thought was to seek her on my return, and try to win her for my wife.'

'It's deuced unfortunate, Rob,' said the other in his nervous way. Then, with a kind of bravado, he continued half laughingly: 'But then, you see, you have been away two years, and you have stopped away too long. It's a pity, too, such friends as we were.'

Ere he had finished speaking his companion had seized his arm as in a vice.

'Huish!' he cried hoarsely, 'if you speak to me in

that tone of voice I will not answer for the conse-
quences. I do not wish to be rash, or to condemn
you unheard ; but this is of such vital import to
me that, by God, if you speak of it in that flippant
tone again, I shall forget that we are gentlemen, and,
like some brute beast, I shall have you by the throat.'

'Loose my arm,' exclaimed the other, flushing
more deeply ; 'you hurt me.'

'You hurt me,' cried the other, trembling with
passion—'to the heart.'

'If I have wronged you,' exclaimed Huish, 'even
if duelling is out of fashion, I can give you satisfaction.'

'Satisfaction !' cried the other bitterly. 'Look
here, James Huish. You have been a man of
fashion, while I have been a blunt soldier. If what
I hear be true, would it be any satisfaction for me to
shoot you through the head, and break that poor
girl's heart, for I could do it if I liked ; and if I did
not, would it be any satisfaction to let you make
yourself a murderer ?'

Huish shuddered slightly, and the colour paled in
his cheeks.

' Now answer my question.   I say, is this true ?'

' We are old friends,' retorted Huish, 'but you have no right to question me.'

' Right or no right, I will question you,' exclaimed the other passionately, 'and answer me you shall before you leave this spot.'

Huish glanced uneasily to the right and left, and, seeing this, his companion laid his hand once more upon his arm.

' No,' he exclaimed, 'you do not go ; and for your own sake, do not provoke me.'

The speaker's voice trembled with rage, which he seemed to be fighting hard to control, while Huish was by turns flushed with anger, and pale with something near akin to fear.

' I will not answer your questions,' he exclaimed desperately.

' You promised me you would, and you shall, James Huish.   Look here, sir.   A little over two years ago there was a servant at the cottage—a cold hard girl.   I come back here, and I find this same girl now a woman.   She recognised me when I met her yesterday, and, believing that I was going

to the cottage, she stopped me, and by degrees told
me such a tale as I would I had never lived to hear.
I went away again yesterday half mad, hardly believing that it could be true. To-day I returned, and
she pointed you out to me as the villain—as Mr.
Ranby—a serpent crawling here to poison under
an assumed name.'

'Go on,' said the other. 'You meant marriage of
course.'

'I tell you, man, I never had a thought for that
poor girl that was not pure and true. If I had
spoken so soon, it might have checked an intercourse
that was to me the happiest of my life. Now I come
back and find that the peace of that little home is
blasted—that the woman I have loved has been
made the toy of your pleasure; that you whom I
believed to be a gentleman, a man of honour, have
proved to be the greatest of villains upon this earth.'

'Have a care what you say,' said Huish hotly.

'I will have a care,' cried the other. 'I will not
condemn you on the words of others; I would not
so condemn the man who was my closest friend.
Speak, then; tell me. I say, is this all true?'

'You have no right to question me.'

'I say, is this true, James Huish?'

'Look here. What is the use of making a fuss like this over a bit of an affair of gallantry.'

'What!' cried the other, grasping the arm of Huish once more tightly. 'An affair of gallantry? Is it, then, an affair of gallantry to come upon a home like a blight—to destroy—yes, blast the life of a pure, trusting, simple-hearted girl, who believes you to be the soul of honour? James Huish, I do not understand these terms; but tell me this,' he continued in a voice that was terrible in its cold measured tones, 'is this true?'

'Is what true?' said the other, with an attempt at bravado.

'You know what I mean—about Mary Riversley.'

'Well, there, yes, I suppose it is,' said Huish, with assumed indifference; 'and now the murder's out.'

'No,' exclaimed the other, with the rage he had been beating down struggling hard for the mastery; 'not murder: it is worse. But look here, Huish. This girl is fatherless,' he continued in a voice quite unnaturally calm. 'I loved her very dearly, but, poor girl, her affection has gone to another. She cannot be my wife, but I can be her friend and I will. You will marry her at once.'

'Not likely,' was the scornful reply, as Huish tried to shake his arm free.

'I say, James Huish, you will marry this poor girl —no, this dear, sweet, injured lady—at once. The world would call her fallen; I say she is a good, true woman, as pure as snow, and in the sight of God Almighty your own wife. But we have customs here in England that must be observed. I say again, you will marry Ruth Riversley—at once?'

'I—will—not!' said Huish slowly and distinctly, the pain he suffered bringing a burning spot in each cheek, and his temper now mastering the dread he felt of his companion.

'I say again,' said the other, in the same strange un-natural tone, 'you will marry Miss Riversley—at once.'

'And I say,' cried Huish, now half mad with rage and pain, 'I will not. Marry her yourself,' he said brutally, 'if——'

'Damned traitor!' cried the other, choking the completion of the sentence, as, active as a panther, he caught Huish by the throat. 'Dog! coward! scoundrel! Down on your knees, and swear you will marry her, or I will not answer for your life!'

Huish in his dread half wrenched himself free, and a wild, strange cry escaped his lips. Then, nerved by his position, he turned upon his assailant, and a deadly struggle commenced.

They were well matched, but the young officer, hardened by a rough life, was the more active, and as they swayed to and fro in a fierce embrace, he more than once seemed on the point of forcing his adversary to the ground; but Huish putting forth his whole strength recovered himself, and the struggle was renewed with greater violence than before.

It was an aimless encounter, such as would result from two men engaging when maddened with rage. Their cheeks were purple, their veins stood out in their temples, and their eyes flashed with the excitement of the encounter. The danger they risked in their proximity to the deep pit was not heeded, and more than once as they wrestled to and fro, they nearly touched the fence that ran along the brink; but neither seemed to be aware of its existence, the short grass and heather by the side of the path was trampled, the bushes rustled and the twigs were broken as the antagonists in turn seemed to gain the mastery, and then for a few moments they paused, each gripping the other tightly, and gazing angrily in one another's eyes.

There was the low sobbing pant of labouring breath, the heaving of strong men's breasts, and then without a word being spoken the struggle recommenced.

It soon became evident that Huish was trying all he could to throw his adversary, the idea uppermost being that if he could get Captain Millet to the ground, he might hold him there till help came. On the other side Millet's main thought was to put into execution his threat; force Huish to his knees, and there make him humbly ask pardon and take such an oath as he should prescribe.

The upshot of the struggle was very different, though, from what either had imagined, and one that strongly influenced their future lives.

As the struggle was resumed, the better training of Millet, who was hard and spare, began to tell upon

Huish, whose life of ease had not fitted him for so arduous an encounter. His breath was drawn heavily, and at rapid intervals; his grasp of his adversary was less firm; the big drops stood upon his face, and a singing noise began to sound in his ears, while the thought which made him feel infuriate seemed about to be realized, and in imagination he saw himself humbled before his friend.

In fact, the latter nearly had him at his mercy as they now swayed to and fro, and tightening his grasp with one hand, he suddenly lowered the other, and catching Huish at a disadvantage, he would in another instant have thrown him, when, maddened by desperation, Huish dashed himself forward to forestall his antagonist's effort, Millet's heel caught in a furze-bush, and the two men fell heavily against the rough fence.

There was a sharp crack made by the breaking wood, the rushing noise of falling earth and stones, and the next moment Huish was clinging to the rough stem of a bunch of golden broom, hanging at arm's length over the gravel-pit, while from beneath him came up a dull, heavy thud as of some fallen body.

Faint, sick, breathless, and ready to loose his
hold, Huish clung there in an agony of desperation
for a few moments. The trees, the clouds above
him, seemed to be whirling round, and he closed his
eyes preparatory to falling in his turn.

Then came the reaction, and, how he afterwards
hardly knew, he made two or three desperate efforts
to find rest for his feet, but only at first to send
down avalanche after avalanche of stones and earth.
Then one foot rested on a piece of old stump, and
he was able to take some of the strain off his arms,
resting there panting, and with a strange creeping
sensation assailing his nerves as he thought that
in a few minutes at most he must fall.

He glanced down once, to see that the stones
were some thirty or forty feet below ; and in his then
position the height seemed dreadful, and with a
shudder he wrenched his gaze away and looked up,
thinking now of escape.

The stem he clung to was pretty strong, but the
shrub was only rooted in the gravelly side of the pit,
and at any moment it might be torn out by his
weight. In fact, it seemed already to be giving way.

But now his breath came in less laboured fashion, and the power to act began to return, the result being that he took in at a glance his situation, and, stretching out one of his feet, he found for it a more secure resting-place, one which enabled him to get hold of a stronger and tougher shrub, and draw himself to where he could stand in comparative safety, with the fence only some five feet above his hands.

Could he reach that, or must he descend?

He glanced down again.

Descent was impossible, for the side of the pit was eaten away by the weather, and receded from him, so once more with a shudder he looked up.

Yes, there was a clump of furze a foot or two higher, just on the edge where the grass reached before the gravel began to recede. Could he reach that?

For a few moments he hesitated to make the attempt—it was so hazardous, for, even should he reach it, the roots might give way. Then, rendered desperate by his position, and feeling sure that his fall must be the work of a few minutes if he stayed where he was, he gathered himself together, drew a long breath, made a tremendous effort, and got hold of the stout stem of the furze-bush, which tore and scarified his wrists. But that was not heeded, and drawing his feet up, he struggled vainly for a few moments to get some place of rest for them, but only for the gravel and stones to keep crumbling away.

Another minute of such effort and he must have fallen. It was only by letting himself hang by his hands with outstretched arms that he could just rest one foot upon a great stone embedded in the face of the pit. Small as it was, though, it was rest, and he remained quiescent once more.

As he hung there with nerves throbbing, and a strange aching sensation beginning to numb his muscles, he felt once more that he must fall, and so overpowering was the thought that he nearly loosened his hold. But the dread of death prevailed, and, making a fresh effort, he drew himself up quickly, gained a hold for the toe of one boot, made a snatch at a root a little higher, then at another, and his feet rested upon the furze stem. Another effort, and he had hold of one of the posts of the open fence, and the next minute he had crawled through the broken portion, struggled to his feet, and sunk down upon the heath, giddy, exhausted and ready to faint.

In a few minutes he had recovered himself, and getting up, he was fain to take off the stout bottom joint of his fly-rod, which, with its spear, made a sturdy support as he went to the edge of the pit, and with a shrinking sensation that he could not master, gazed down below.

He turned shuddering away, and walked a dozen paces to where he could made his way down through the trees to the bottom of a slope, where, parting the bushes, he directly after stood in the cart-track, now grown over with grass and heather, but which had once been the way used by those who carted the gravel.

His giddiness wore off, and gave place to a terrible feeling of dread as he walked hastily on, parting at last some low-growing twigs of birch, to stand beside the prostrate body of his adversary.

Millet was lying upon his back with one leg bent under him, and his arm in an unnatural position, and as James Huish gazed down upon him, the horrible thought occurred to him that the end of his affair of gallantry, as he termed it, might be a trial for murder.

As this thought presented itself, bitter repentance attacked him ; his knees shook beneath him, and at last he fell upon them beside the body of his former friend, to moan in agony.

' God help me, what have I done ?'

He took the fallen man's hand, and laid the arm in a natural position.

It was broken.

He then tried to lay his leg in its normal place, but there was something wrong; he could not tell what. And now he did what he might have been expected to do first, laid his hand upon the breast to try and find out if the injured man still lived.

He started to his feet then with the cold perspiration bedewing his forehead, and gazing sharply round, he exclaimed :

' I call Heaven to witness I never meant him harm.'

Then, throwing himself upon his knees, he began to examine the injured man once more, with feverish haste tearing open his shirt-front, laying his ear close to his lips, and ending by scooping up some clear water with both his hands from a little pool hard by, and dashing it in the prostrate man's face.

'I little thought it would come to this. Rob— can you hear me? My God!' he groaned, 'he must be dead.'

At that moment, to his great joy, the injured man moaned slightly, and, to Huish's great relief, at last opened his eyes, and gazed vacantly round.

'Can you drink some of this?' said Huish eagerly, as he unscrewed the top of a small flask, and held it to the other's lips.

Millet swallowed a few drops, and soon the vacant look passed from his eyes, and he groaned heavily.

'Huish,' he said hoarsely. 'You've given me—my death-blow—hope first—now my life.'

'No, no—no, no!' exclaimed Huish. 'Can you bear for me to leave you now? I'll run for help.'

'Stop,' exclaimed Millet, making an effort to rise, and sinking back with a groan of agony. 'Stop! come closer.'

Huish obeyed, and held the flask once more to his lips, but it was pushed aside.

'Is this manslaughter or murder?' he said, with a bitter smile.

'I protest to heaven,' began Huish.

'Hush! Listen! That poor girl—Mary—now—quick, at once—swear to me by all you hold sacred—you will—at once—make her your wife.'

Millet's face was ghastly pale, and he spoke with difficulty, but one hand now grasped the wrist of Huish with a firm hold, and his eyes were fixed upon those of the man who bent over him with feverish intensity.

'Yes, yes, I will—on my soul, I will,' cried Huish, with frantic vehemence. 'Rob, old fellow, if I could undo——'

'You cannot. Quick, man; swear it—you will marry her—at once.'

'I swear I will,' cried Huish.

'So help you God.'

'So help me, God!' exclaimed Huish, 'and help me now,' he added in agony, 'for he is dying.'

'Here—below there—Hi!' shouted a voice from the pathway above. 'What's the matter?'

'Quick, quick, help!' cried Huish, and his appeal was answered by rapid footsteps, the rustling of bushes, and directly after, a short, broad-shouldered young man, with a large head and keen gray eyes, was at his side.

'I say,' he cried; 'struggle up above, broken fence, man killed!'

Huish started back, staring at him with dilated eyes, and then by an effort he exclaimed:

'Quick—run—the nearest doctor, man.'

'Six miles away,' was the sharp reply. 'I'm a sucker—medical stoo,' he added; and pulling off his coat, he rapidly rolled it into a pad for a pillow before proceeding in a business-like way to examine the fallen man's injuries. 'I say, this is bad—arm broken—hip joint out—hold still, old fellow, I won't hurt you,' he said, as his patient moaned. 'You'd better go for help. I'll stay. Leave me that flask; and, I say, just see if my fishing tackle's all right: I left it up at the top.' Then, as if inspired by the words uttered by the injured man a few minutes before, he exclaimed : 'I say, I don't know that I ought to let you go; is this manslaughter or murder ?'

' No,' moaned Millet, unclosing his eyes, and speaking in a hoarse whisper—' my old friend—an accident—sir—an accident.'

'I say, the brandy, man, the brandy,' cried the new-comer. 'By Jove he's fainted.'

' He's dead—he's dead,' groaned Huish frantically, as he sank upon his knees and caught his friend's hand. 'Rob, old fellow, I'd give my life that this had not happened; but I'll keep my word; I'll keep my word.'

CHAPTER III.

FOSTER-PARENTS.

As Jane Glyne said, just four miles away from The
Dingle was a low, long range of hovels, roughly built
in the coarsest manner, and so covered in that but for
a stuffing of straw here and there, the bleak winds
and rain that come even in summer could beat
through with all their force.

The hovels were built on the unity principle—one
room—one door—one chimney—one window, and
they stood in a row close by the bank of a canal
which formed the great highway to and from the
dirty Goshen of these modern children of Israel.

But they were not Jews, any more than they were
Christians: they were simply work-people — the
slaves who make bricks without straw, and not for
the use of a king of Egypt, but for modern Babylon.

The canal was the great highway to this settlement, which stood in an earth-gnawed desert of its own; but all the same there was a rugged pathway which led towards the pretty stream on whose bank stood Mrs. Riversley's cottage, passable in fine weather, a slough in wet; and there was a roadway for carts, a horribly churned up mingling of mud and water, along which chariot wheels drave heavily to work woe upon that patient martyr of ours — the horse.

It was not a pleasant spot that brick-field, and seemed to have been thrust out far from the habitations of ordinary men. It was not salubrious, but then its subsoil was of the stiffest clay. Here the brickmakers lived gregariously, each hovel containing as many as it would hold. Here four or five men 'pigged' together. It was their own term, and most appropriate. In another hovel, a young couple would have three young men lodgers, while the occupants of other dens would have done the same, only that their swarming children did not give room for lodgers to lie down, the superficies of the floors being small.

A desolate-looking spot on a flat expanse, through which the canal, erst a river, ran. It was once a series of pleasant meadows, but Babylon swallows many bricks. Hence the tract had been delved all over into a chaos of clay, where long rows of bricks stood drying, while others were being made. Stagnant water covered with green scum lay in the holes whence clay had been dug, while other holes were full of liquid mud. Dirt-pie-making by horse-power seemed to be going on all day long, and soft mud mixtures were formed, water being run into banked-up lakes by means of wooden troughs, while every here and there wretched horses, blindfolded so that they should not resent their task, seemed to be turning torture machines to break up so much obstinate clay upon the wheel.

The breeze there was not a balmy wind, laden with sweet floral odours, but a solid gritty breeze, being the musty, ill-savoured, sifted ashes of the great city, brought in processions of barges to mix with the clay, to be burned and go back as so much brick.

'Bring that bairn here,' cried a shrill voice, proceeding from a being, who, but for the shaping of the

scanty garment she had on, might have been taken
for a clay-daubed man. Her long cotton dress clung
close to her figure, for it was soaked with water, and
on ' that bairn,' a tiny little morsel whose experience
of the world was not many hours old, being brought to
her by a half-naked girl of ten with something cotton
upon her, but more clay, the infant was tended in
a maternal way for some little time, during which
the woman, as she rocked herself to and fro, made
use of an unoccupied hand to draw a piece of
rag from her pocket, and then, much to the dis-
comfort of the infant, she tied up in the corners and
middle of the rag, with as many knots, five new,
bright sovereigns.

' Look out, mother,' cried the girl, but her warning
came too late : a heavy-looking man in half a shirt,
and a pair of trousers held up by a strap, and
who seemed to go by machinery, for he emitted
puffs of smoke from a short black pipe as he moved,
made a snatch at the rag, and thrust it into his
pocket.

' I'll take care o' that 'ere,' he growled ; and, as
the woman uttered a resentful cry, he ' made an

offer' at her with the back of his hand, and then began puffing smoke once more, and moved away. The woman cowered down to avoid the expected blow, muttered viciously to herself, and at last rose, and tucked the babe into an improvised bed of rags in the shelter of a shed. This, by the way, was only a sloping roof of boards some six feet by five, covering the rough bench upon which a brickmaker works, and being unoccupied just then, came in handy for the purpose to which it was put.

'I'll have that back agen, old man,' the woman muttered to herself. 'Just wait till you're asleep. Now then,' she cried aloud to sundry clayey imps who were at work fetching and carrying the plastic mass with which they were daubed, 'keep a hye on this bairn, all on yer. If Bill Jones's dawg comes anigh, let go at him.'

Saying this, she joined 'father,' who under the next shed was puffing away as he worked, a puff being emitted as each brick was made in its mould, and turned out upon a board.

'When's she comin' agen about that there kid?' growled father.

'Wait and see,' said the woman surlily, as she attacked a mass of clay, as if it were so much dough, pinched off pieces, and roughly shaped them into loaves a little larger than a brick ready for the man to mould.

Then there was a pause, during which the puffs of smoke came with beautiful regularity from the brickmaker's mouth, and as a boy approached, it almost seemed as if he were going to stoke father, and put on some more coals ; but he only dabbed down a mass of clay which he had carried upon his head, whose shape was printed in the lump which left a portion amongst the boy's hair.

'Think it were Bill Jones's dawg as took Lamby's kid, mother ?' growled father at last.

'Think ? I'm sure on it,' said mother. 'It were there one minute, and it were gone the next. Where could it ha' gone if he hadn't took it.'

The machinery stopped, for father took his pipe out of his mouth, wiped his lips with the back of his clayey hand, which was all the cleaner afterwards, father's lips having the character of a short stubbly bristled brush. Then he thought for a minute ; the machinery began to go once more, a puff of smoke was emitted from his lips and he replied:

' Dunno !'

' I think Lamby's gal, July, dropped it in the canal, and was 'fraid to tell,' said the girl in the clay robe shrilly.

'You hold your noise, and look alive wi' them lumps,' growled father, who made as if to strike the girl, whereupon she ducked down to avoid the expected blow, dodged away to a safe distance, put out her tongue, and said, 'Yah!' and the other children —four—all engaged in carrying clay, laughed and ran to avoid blows.

They varied in age from five to fourteen, and were all richly clothed in clay, which coated them from their hair—tangled and hardened with the worked-up adhesive soil—to their very toes, which printed their shapes in the moist ground they trod.

Father seeming disposed to 'hull' one of the moulds at them, they all hastened away to the clay mill—a machine like a great churn bound with many strong iron hoops and with a thumper or plunger therein, to which a long wooden bar was attached, harnessed to one end of which was another blindfolded skeleton of a horse, which still retained its skin and vitality, and went round and round despondently, as if under the impression that it was going straight forward; but a sharp jerk of the head seemed to say from time to time: ' It doesn't matter; it will not be for long.'

At the bottom of the great mill, in a gloomy hole, was a clayey man in a kind of rough apron, and armed with a piece of wire two feet long, whose ends were twisted round a couple of pieces of wood to form handles.

As the mill turned, the well-mixed clay was forced through the bottom in a mass some ten inches in diameter, which from time to time the man dexterously cut through with his wire, and passed the pieces to the children who came for fresh supplies.

One took the heavy fat lump, and hugged it to its breast, making a mould in the top for its little chin. Another had it dabbed upon its curly head; another bore it upon the shoulder, leaving therein the print of the ear; but the favourite way seemed to be to hug it to the breast back to the shed, where mother seized it and went on making her brown loaves.

Father, whose external machinery consisted of some water, some dry, sandy earth, and a little oblong box the shape of the brick, seized the brown loaves his wife passed to him, gave them a dexterous dab which forced them into the mould, scraped off the top level with the sides, pushed it along on a board, raised the mould, and left there a soft clay brick.

Then with regular puffs the process was repeated again and again, while a man with a strange-shaped barrow removed the new soft bricks and bore them away.

At the first sight it seemed as if the babe Jane Glyne had brought had fallen amongst savages, but they were English fellow-creatures, living—existing rather—not so very far from the centre of civilization, and——bricks are in great demand.

As the work went on in its muddy monotony, an evil-looking, long-jawed dog, the very opposite of the hound in the legend who slew the wolf to save his master's child, came slinking and sniffing about

the sheds. He was a lean, starving, wolfish, mangy
cur, with reddish glaring eyes, always on the watch
for kicks and blows. He would have been a big dog
had he been fed, but want of food appeared to have
produced a bad crop of hair upon his skin, and given
him a thin shadowy look even to his head, which
seemed to have been starved into a snarl and a set
of teeth.

The dog slunk here and slunk there for a time, till
his keen senses led him towards where, some fifty
yards away, one of the brickmakers' dinners lay
within his reach. Giving a sharp glance round, he
had already opened his sharp jaws to snatch up the
knotted handkerchief which held a basin, when a
well-aimed, half-dried brick struck him in the ribs,
which emitted a cavernous drummy sound, and with
a sharp yelp the brute bounded off.

But he was too hungry to be driven right away,
and before long he stopped short, screwed himself
round, and soothed the injured spot with half a dozen
licks. Then, wild of eye and wolfish of aspect, he
turned once more towards the sheds to seek for food.

He whined a little, either from pain or from an

injured feeling—his *amour propre* telling him that dogs must live as well as the savages round whose camp he prowled.   Then, forgetting one pain external in a greater one within, he set off once more, but this time displaying a caution worthy of a wolf as he neared the shed where father, mother, and the clayey children were all so busily at work making their summer harvest—too busy to mind the wretched foster-child, which, after feebly appealing against the neglect, and turning its little face to and fro in search of something warm, had gone off fast asleep.

CHAPTER IV.

INOCULATED FOR A WOLF.

SUDDENLY in the midst of the work there was the sound of a whip cracking, accompanied by loud oaths, many of them very red, shouts, and the jerking noise of chain harness.

It was nothing new, but being a diversion from the monotony of their work, half the brickmakers stopped to look on.

The remnant of a fine horse was in the shafts of a heavily-laden sand cart, which he had dragged for some distance through the tenacious mud of the deeply-cut ruts, till, coming to a softer place than usual, one wheel had gone down nearly to the nave in the mire, tilting the cart sideways, and every frantic struggle made by the poor beast only seemed

4—2

to set it more fast. Its hoofs, which sank deeply,
churned up the mud and water, and it stood still at
last with heaving flanks, its great earnest eyes staring
appealingly at its masters, while the blindfolded
skeleton in the clay mill went round and round, then
stopped short, and gave its head a jerk, as if saying
once more, 'It doesn't matter; it will not be for
long.'

Click, clack, clack went the whip, and the skeleton
in the mill started energetically once more, while the
horse in the cart struggled spasmodically to move
the load, much of its strength being, however, exhausted by extricating its hoofs from the clayey,
sticky mud.

Click, clack, clack went the whip once more, and as
Jane Glyne came along panting and perspiring with
the weight of her bundle, a little crowd of clayey
savages began to collect.

The horse struggled with a piteous expression in
the wrinkles above its starting eyes; its flanks
heaved; they moistened the lash of the cruel whip,
and still it strove; but the cart wheels had sunk
so low that a team could hardly have dragged it out,

and the willing beast vainly essayed the impossible. A dozen strong men stood around, as many shovels were within reach ready to remove the clay from the wheels, and partially dig them out ; but, as Jane Glyne looked on, in a strange, hard, callous manner, no one made a move, not a hand was placed to a wheel-spoke to help with a few pounds the labouring beast. Cartloads of hard broken brick rubbish lay about that could have been thrown down to fill up the ruts ; but not a barrowful was brought, and amidst a shower of oaths, there was added, to make it a storm, a shower of blows.

The horse's struggles grew interesting, and as the little crowd increased pipes were replenished, and the heavy clay-sullied men looked on.

More blows, more struggles ; but the cart sank deeper, and was not likely to be moved, for, in spite of the frantic way in which the horse plunged into its collar, it could not stir the load an inch. Not an inch, strong as it was ; but there is exhaustion even for the strongest, and at last the poor brute stood deep in the tenacious mud, with wet heaving flanks, staring eyes, and trembling in every limb.

' Here, give us holt !' cried father; and his children brought up in this earthly school looked on with glee.

' Father 'll soon fetch him out,' said the eldest boy; and it seemed that at last the poor brute was to get some help.   But it was not help the horse was to have, for the whip was handed to father.

' Take holt on his head,' he cried to the man in charge, and the latter ruffian seized the rein, and began to jerk and drag the bit savagely.

' Jeet—jeet—aw—a—a—ya ! Hoot !' roared the ruffian, with a hot burst of oaths, while father, puffing regularly his smoke, turned his machinery to bear upon the poor dumb brute, and with a grim smile lashed and cut at it, ingeniously seeking out the tender parts beneath.

' Gie't 'im, lad.   Gie't 'im,' rose in chorus.

The poor trembling horse, roused by the stinging thong, shot into the collar in a way that broke one of the chains that linked it to the shaft, and then as a more cruel lash fell upon its side, it fell upon its knees, the cart shafts pinning it down as the load sank forward.   Now followed more lashing, the horse struggled frantically, rolled over, dragging its legs from the mud, plunged and struck out as if galloping, though its hoofs only beat the mud and water. Then it raised its head two or three times as if trying to regain its feet, before letting it subside into the mud, and the eye that was visible began to roll.

' Get up !' roared father, with a burst of oaths, and again the whip came into play.

But it was an order that the poor brute, willing to the last, could not obey, pinned down as it was by the shafts and the weight of the sand. At the first cut of the whip, though, the horse struck out with its hoofs, sending the mud flying, and causing a roar of laughter amongst the crowd as father was bespattered from head to foot. Then there was a curious gasping cry as the horse threw up its head; a shiver ran through its heaving frame ; a couple of jets of blood started from its nostrils ; there was a strange sigh, and the head fell heavily down in the mud and water.

Even then there was a sharp lash given with the whip, just as a convulsive kick or two splashed up the mud, before the willing beast lay motionless ; it had

broken its heart—no metaphor here for excess of
sorrow, but the simple truth, while the listening
skeleton in the mill gave its head another jerk, and
seemed to say, 'I knew it wouldn't be for long.'

'Well——'

Father did not finish his sentence, for Jane Glyne
uttered a loud shriek and dropped her bundle in the
mud just as a shout arose from one of father's clay-
daubed sons.

'Hi! chivy him,' roared the boy. 'Bill Jones's
dawg has got that kid.'

It was too true: the wolfish starveling beast had
watched his opportunity while the crowd was
occupied, slinked up to the shed, seized the babe by
one arm, and was stealing cautiously off, when the
boy turned and saw him, shouted, gave chase, and
the savage brute broke into a heavy lumbering
canter.

For a short distance he dragged the child along
the earth; then, with a dexterous twist, he threw
it over his shoulders and increased his pace.

'Hi! stop him, hi!' roared a score of voices which
echoed through the brickfield, and men, women, and

children came hurrying from all parts to take up the chase.

For they saw in a moment what had taken place, and the hunt roused all to a pitch of excitement consequent upon the evil reputation borne by 'Bill Jones's dawg.'

This being the case, the way off to the open fields where the woodland and stream lay beyond the flat plain was closed, and for a moment or two the dog halted and threw up his head to see that he was hemmed in on three sides by enemies, while at his back was the canal, and for water he had no love.

Enemies they were indeed, for the brickfield savages were human, after all, and every man, woman, and child was armed with shovel, stick, or well-burned fragment of refuse brick—this last, a missile that he knew by heart as angular and sharp ; and dog as he was, he had sense enough to feel that, if taken, they would pound the life out of his wretched carcase on the spot.

If he had dropped his prey, he might have shown his pursuers a clean pair of heels ; but he was hungry—wolfishly hungry, and more savage than domestic as he was, he literally knew the taste of that which he held between his teeth. He would have died the death before, on suspicion, had not Bill, his master, interposed. Now, however, he saw the said Bill armed with a clay spade, although he whistled to him to come. But 'Bill Jones's dawg' knew too well the treachery of the human heart, and would not listen to whistle nor following call.

Which way should he go? Towards that frantic woman who had torn off her shawl? No. There was the clinker kiln, where a whole burning of bricks was spoiled. He could not reach the open—he would have been cut off as he went, and chopped with spades, and stunned with brick-bats; but there was that kiln standing old and weather-beaten, a very sanctuary of bricks burned into solid masses, full in view, though a quarter of a mile lower by the other works. Yes, there was that kiln abounding in convenient holes, where he had often spent the night; he might reach there in safety with his prey, and then——

'Hi! stop him—stop him!'

The yelling crowd was closing in and growing more dangerous every moment, so the dog took a tighter grip of his prize, and made straight for the old kiln.

Brickmaking was impossible in the face of such a chase, and everyone joined in, with the full determination that this day ' Bill Jones's dawg ' must die.

' Hi! stop him—stop him !'

By an ingenious double or two, the dog nearly reached the refuge that he sought, but he was cut off and turned back by swift-footed boys, yelling with excitement and panting to hurl the first lump of brick at the hated beast. But the dog kept out of harm's way by running between the rows of piled-up, unburnt bricks, which afforded him shelter, and the baby, too, for missiles went flying after them at every chance.

Up this row, down that, and zigzag to and fro, till the canal was near, and the forces joining, the dog was nearly driven to leap into the foul stagnant water ; but again he doubled, passed through an opening, and was once more in the shelter between two rows of bricks, cantering along towards the end.

Here, though, he was cut off again by one of the lads, who, divining the course he had taken, shouted to part of the contingent, and turned the wily brute back.

But he was not beaten. He was starving, but he was hard and strong: no fattened, asthmatic favourite was he, but long-winded and lank, ready to run for an hour yet, even with the load he bore. Wily too, as his relative the fox, he cleverly doubled in and out, in the maze-like rows of wet bricks, avoiding as if by magic the missiles that were thrown; and at last, just as the boys were driving him back towards the spade-armed men, whom he had from the first given a wide berth, he cleverly dashed for the weak part in the advancing line of lads, passed them, put on all his pace, and went away for the kiln.

There were swift runners amongst those lightly-clad, barefooted boys, and now that it had become a tail race, away they went with all their might, faster and faster, and yelling till they were hoarse. For there were shouts and cries of encouragement from behind, enough to spur on the greatest laggard, and

on they went till the dog reached the old kiln and
tried to enter a low hole, probably the one he made
his den.

Here, though, he had a check, by the clothes of
the infant catching in the rough scoria, when—fox-
like—he backed out, turned, and then began to back
in.

That momentary check saved the child: for just as
it was disappearing in the opening, the foremost boy
bounded up, caught the infant by its leg, and the
long robe it wore, and, pulling and shouting hard,
succeeded in drawing the wretched little object back,
the dog snarling savagely, and holding on with all his
might; but just then half a brick smote him on the
head, he loosed his hold, and, backing in, the child
with its lacerated arm and shoulder was held up on
high amidst the cheering of the boys.

In another minute the panting crowd surrounded
the opening, and Jane Glyne had the baby in her
arms, wondering whether it was alive or dead.

The tragedy was not over yet.

Bill Jones stood amongst the men, and was for
defending his 'dawg,' but the blood of all present

was thoroughly roused, and though Bill declared his readiness to fight any man present for a pot, he soon cried off on finding that his challenge was taken up by a score of fellow-workers, half of whom began to prepare for the trial by battle on the spot.

'I don't keer what you do wi' the dawg,' Bill growled, taking out and beginning to fill his pipe, and directly after joining in the attempt about to be made to get the beast out of his place of refuge.

Forming themselves into a semicircle round the opening, a part stood ready, while some of the sturdiest brickmakers began to drag the burrs apart, a task in which they had not been long engaged, standing upon the heap, before there was a rustling noise; the old rough bricks began to crumble down inwards; and with a savage snarl the frightened dog bounded out.

There was a shout, a chorus of yells, mingled with which was the last ever given by 'Bill Jones's dawg,' for his mortal race was run. Even Cerberus of the three heads could not have existed many seconds beneath the shower of bricks and clinkers that assailed him after the savage chop given by father's spade. One yell only, and there was a mass of brick rising over him, the dog's death and burial being a simultaneous act on the part of those who, old and young, did not pause until they had erected a rough but respectable mausoleum over the wolfish creature's grave.

'Put a bit o' wet 'bacco on the place,' said father, removing his pipe as he turned to where Jane Glyne and mother were examining the little frail morsel, which, in spite of its usage, began now to wail feebly; 'put a bit o' wet 'bacco on the place; it ain't dead. There, give it to mother; and, I say, when are you going to pay agen?'

'Never,' cried Jane Glyne, hastily wrapping the baby in the shawl now handed by one of the staring girls.

'Oh, it ain't hurt much,' said father; 'put a bit o' wet 'bacco on the place.'

'Hurt!' cried the woman excitedly, as with a newly-awakened interest she held the child tightly to her hard breast, 'it's a'most killed, and if it lives, that dog's teeth have poisoned it, and it will go mad.'

' Not it,' growled father ; ' why, the dawg is dead. Give it to mother, and I say, when——why, she's gone !'

He said this after a pause, as he stared after Jane Glyne hurrying towards the path where her bundle lay, but thinking more of her little burden, inoculated by the poison of those wolfish teeth—blood-poisoned, perhaps, as to its mental or bodily state—certainly suffering from lacerations that might end its feeble little life.

———◆———

CHAPTER I.

CINDERELLA AND THE SISTERS.

' RUTH.'

' Yes, dear; I'll come directly.'

' Ruth !'

' Be quiet, Clo. She can't come yet.'

' But she must come. Ruth !'

' May I go to her, Marie ?'

' No, certainly not. Finish my hair first.'

Two pretty little white patient hands went on busying themselves plaiting the rich dark-brown hair of a singularly handsome girl, sitting back in a shabby, painted, rush-bottomed chair, in a meanly-furnished chamber, whose bare boards looked the more chilly for the scraps of carpet stretched by bedside, toilet-table, and washstand.

The bed had not long been left, and the two pillows each bore the impress of a head. The bedstead was an attenuated four-post structure, with dreary and scanty slate-coloured hangings, that seemed to have shrunk in their many washings, and grown skimpy and faded with time; the rush-bottomed chairs were worn and the seats giving way, and a tall painted wardrobe had been scrubbed until half the paint had gone. Even the looking-glass upon the paltry old dressing-table seemed to have reflected until it could perform its duties no more, for the silver had come off in patches, and showed the bare brown wood behind.

Wherever the eye rested it was upon traces of cleanly, punctilious poverty, for even the dresses that were hanging from the row of drab-painted wooden pegs nailed against the dreary washed-out wall-paper looked mean and in keeping with the room. There was not one single attractive object of furniture or attire besides, not even a bright spring flower in a vase or glass ; all was drab, dreary, and dull, and yet the room and objects full of life and light.

For the girl seated indolently in the chair before the glass, draped in a long washed-out dressing-gown that heightened rather than hid the graces of her well-developed form, possessed features which might have been envied by a queen. Her dark, well-arched eyebrows, the long heavy lashes that drooped over her large eyes, her creamy complexion, rather full but well-cut lips and high brow, were all those of a beautiful woman whom you would expect to look imperious and passionate if she started into motion, and raised and flashed upon you the eyes that were intent upon a paper-covered French novel, whose leaves she turned over from time to time.

Bending over her, and nimbly arranging the rich hair that hung over the reader's shoulders, was a girl not unlike her in feature, but of a fairer and more English type. Where the hair of the one was rich and dark, that of the other was soft and brown. The contour was much the same, but softer, and the eyes were of that delicious well-marked gray that accords so well with light nut-brown hair. There

was no imperious look in her pleasant, girlish countenance, for it was full of care consequent upon her
being wanted in two places at once.

For the sharp demand made upon her was uttered
by a third occupant of the room—a girl of one or
two and twenty, sister, without doubt, of the reader
at the dressing-table, and greatly like her, but darker,
her eyebrows and hair being nearly black, her complexion of a richer creamy hue, one which seemed
to indicate the possibility of other than English
blood being mingled in her veins.

She, too, was draped in a long washed-out print
dressing-gown, and as she lolled upon a great box
whose top was thinly stuffed and covered with chintz
to make it do duty for an ottoman, her long dark
hair fell in masses over her shoulders.

Sisters undoubtedly, and the family resemblance
of the fair-complexioned girl suggested the possibility
of her occupying the same relationship, though the
difference was so marked that cousin seemed more
probable.

'Finish your own hair,' cried the girl upon the
ottoman, in an angry voice. 'I won't wait any longer;

I was up first;' and she banged down the circulating library novel she had been skimming.

'Shan't !'

'Bring my hairbrush, Ruth.'

The girl addressed retained her hold of the massive plait that she was forming, and, snatching a well-worn hairbrush from the table, reached out as far as she could from the tether of plait that held her to the girl in the chair, when the brush was snatched from her, and sent whizzing through the air, narrowly missing the reader's head, but putting an end to the reflective troubles of the unfortunate toilet-glass, which was struck right in the centre, and shivered into fragments.

'Oh !' ejaculated Ruth.

'Beast !' cried Marie, leaping up, sending her chair backwards, and dashing the French novel at her sister.

'Wretch! devil !' retorted the other, her creamy face flushing, her dark eyes scintillating with passion, and her ruddy lips parting from her regular white teeth, as she retaliated by throwing the book she held, but with a very bad aim.

For a moment it seemed as if blows were to follow, but after a short skirmish with a comb, an empty scent-bottle, and a pin-cushion, the beginner of the fight uttered a cry of triumph, and pounced upon the French novel.

' I wanted that,' she cried.

' Ruth, fetch back that book,' cried Marie.

' Please give me that book back, Clotilde,' said the obedient girl, as, crossing the room, she held out her hand to the angry beauty.

For answer, the maiden upon the box caught her by the wrist with both hands, bent her head rapidly down, and fixed her white teeth in the soft, round arm.

' There, take that, and I wish it was 'Rie's. Now you stop here, and do my hair directly. Hateful little beast ! why didn't you come before ?'

The blood flushed up in Ruth's face, and little troubled lines made their appearance in her fore-head as, after a piteous glance at the other sister, she began to brush the great flowing bands of dark hair waiting their turn.

' I don't care,' said Marie, with all the aggravating petulance of a child. 'Mine was just done.'

'But I've got the book,' retorted the other. 'Be careful, little beast ; don't pull it out by the roots.'

She turned her face up sharply to the busy toiler, with the effect that she dragged her own hair, and this time she struck the girl so sharply on the cheek with the open hand that the tears started to her eyes.

'Nasty, spiteful, malicious wretch!' said Marie, giving the finishing touches to her own hair ; 'but you'll have a good lecture for breaking the glass. Aunties will be angry.'

'I shall say Ruth did it,' said the girl.

'Just like you, Clo,' retorted the other.

'If you call me Clo again, I'll—I'll poison you.'

'Shall if I like : Clo, old Clo—Jew—Jew—Jew ! There !'

As she spoke, Marie turned her mocking coun- tenance to her sister, and finished off by making what children call 'a face,' by screwing up her mouth and nose ; desisting, however, as Clotilde made a dash at the water-glass to throw it at her head, and then made a feint of spitting at her in a feline way.

The whole affair seemed to be more the quarrel of vulgar, spoiled children of nine or ten than an encounter between a couple of grown women in the springtide of their youth, and Ruth silently glanced from one to the other with a troubled, half-pitying expression of countenance; but she did not speak until the noise had begun to lull.

'Please don't say that I broke the glass,' she said at last.

'I shall. Hold your tongue, miss. She broke it through her wretched carelessness, didn't she, 'Rie?'

'Give me back the French book, and I'll tell you,' was the reply.

'Take your nasty old French book,' said Clotilde, throwing it back. 'I've read it all, and it's horribly naughty. Now, then, didn't she break the glass?'

'Yes,' said Marie, arranging her shabby morning dress, and standing before the fragments of the toilet glass, a handsome, lady-like girl, whose beauty no shabbiness of costume could conceal.

' There,' said Clotilde, ' do you hear, Cindy ? You broke the glass, and if you say you didn't I'll make your wretched little life miserable.'

' Very well, dear, I'll say I did,' said Ruth calmly.

' Hist, 'Rie! The book !' whispered Clotilde, her sharp ears having detected a coming step.

Marie made a pantherine bound across the room, and thrust the book between the mattress and paillasse just as the handle rattled, and a tall, gaunt elderly woman entered the room.

She was not pleasant to look upon, for there was too much suggestion of a draped scaffold erected for the building of a female human figure about her hard square bony form, while her hard face, which seemed to wrinkle only about the forehead, as if it had never smiled since childhood, was not made more pleasant by the depth and darkness of the lines in her brow all being suggestive of the soap and flannel never probing their depths, which was not the case, however, for she was scrupulously clean, even to her blonde cap, and its side whiskers with a sad-coloured flower in each.

' Morning, children,' she said harshly. ' Your

aunts 'll be down directly. You ought to be dressed by now.'

' Morning, nurse,' said the girls in chorus.

' Ruth's so slow,' said Clotilde.

' Then do your hair yourself,' said the woman roughly. ' Ruth, child, turn down that bed, and open the window.'

Their actions before her arrival had been those of children ; she treated them like children, and they were as obedient and demure now as little girls, while the woman placed a large white jug containing a tablespoon upon the table, and a plain tumbler beside it.

Ruth began to open the bed, and Marie cast anxious eyes at the part where her French novel lay *perdu.*

' 'Tisn't physic morning again, nurse,' said Clotilde pettishly.

' Yes it is, miss, so don't you grumble. You know it's Wednesday as well as I do.'

Clotilde turned her head away, and gave her teeth an angry snap as she went on rapidly dressing, while the new arrival poured out half a tumbler of a dark-brown fluid from the jug, after giving the said jug a twirl round to amalgamate its contents. This tumbler was handed to Clotilde.

'I'm not ready, nurse,' she said pettishly; 'leave it on the table, and we'll take it. We shall be down directly.'

'I don't go till I can tell your aunts that every drop's taken,' said the woman sturdily. 'I know your tricks, making Miss Ruth drink it all. Both of you did last time.'

'Did Ruth dare to say we did?' cried Marie sharply.

'No, she didn't, miss, so don't you go in a pet.'

'Then how could you tell?' cried Clotilde.

'How could I tell, big baby?' said the woman scornfully; 'why, wouldn't three doses make her ill?'

'I don't know. Ugh! filthy stuff!' said Clotilde, taking the tumbler, drinking off the brown draught, and shuddering afterwards. She set down the glass, which was, after another flourish of the white jug, the spoon being held captive by the woman's thumb, half filled again.

'Now, Miss Marie.'

Marie made a grimace, and drank her portion in turn, after which Ruth swallowed hers with the patience and long-suffering of custom.

' Now, Miss Clotilde,' said the woman, picking out something dark from the bottom of the jug with the spoon, ' here's your prune.'

This was held out in the spoon, and it was ludicrous to see the handsome, womanly girl open her ruddy lips to admit the brown swollen morsel, a similar process being gone through with Marie and Ruth.

' There, children, don't make such a fuss about it,' said the woman. ' It's lucky for you that you've got aunties who take such care of you. Pretty skins and complexions you'd have if you weren't looked after, and when you grow up, if you're wise, you'll treat yourselves just the same. Now then, make haste down.'

This was uttered as she left the room and closed the door, after which Clotilde waited till her steps were inaudible, when she stamped with both her feet, and ground her teeth like an angry child.

' Oh, oh, oh !' she cried. ' The disgusting, filthy stuff. I'm sick of it all, 'Rie. I'll run away with the first man who asks me, even if he's a sweep. I hate it ; I hate everything ; I hate myself, and won't submit any longer. We're not children, and I won't have it. Where's our spirit, that we don't rebel ?'

'Where could we go ? What could we do ?' replied Marie. ' It's horrible. How could we bear it all these weary years ?'

She clasped her hands, and threw herself into her chair, rocking herself to and fro, while Ruth crept softly to her side, and placed her blonde face against the riper, rounder cheek of her cousin.

It was a mute way of showing her sympathy, and Marie felt it to be so, for she turned quickly and kissed her just as the loud jangle of a large hand-bell was heard from below, and Clotilde returned from the open window.

' Come down, girls,' she said bitterly ; 'there's the bell. Old Markes didn't see the broken glass. Go on, Ruthy, and let's get prayers over, or you'll be afraid to tell that fib.'

The bell was still clanging as the three girls went down the one flight of stairs contained in their aunts' share of the private apartments at Hampton

Court, at the bottom of which stairs a tall, thin young man, in a striped jacket, was frantically swinging the noisy instrument to and fro—having to stop, though, to allow the young ladies to pass, when he set down the bell with a clang upon the hearthstoned floor in a dark corner, fiercely dragged a form from under the stairs, and carried it into the dining-room.

It was a brilliant morning in May, but the one window of that dark room received none of the sunshine, for it looked north, over a festive-looking yard or quadrangle, whose stones were mossy and green, kept comfortably damp by their proximity to a basin of water, out of which spurts of water rose from what looked like pieces of black gaspipe ; while three bloated gold and two silver fish swam solemnly round and round, gaping placidly, and staring with apoplectic eyes upwards at the strange phenomenon of what must have seemed to them like a constant shower of rain.

The room was lofty, and panelled in regular compartments, all painted a pale drab, as were also the sides of the floor where the well-worn, indescribable-patterned carpet did not reach; and over this painted portion chairlegs gave uncomfortable scroops.

It was a depressing room, without a particle of ornament, and would have produced indigestion in the healthiest subject. There was a circular sideboard at one end, upon which stood a solemn-looking lamp, whose globe made a dismal boom like a funeral knell when it was removed. Twelve spindly-legged chairs covered with chintz of a washed-out material stood stiffly against the walls, and there were two uneasy chairs covered with chintz and very angular in their backs on either side of the fire, where hung a pair of old-fashioned brass bellows and a worn-out telescope toasting-fork.

As the young ladies entered the room, looking as prim and demure as the chintz-covered chairs, a thin sharp cough was heard on the stairs, followed immediately by another thin sharp cough like the echo of the first, and two very tall meagre ladies entered the room.

Each was dressed in a pale washed-out fabric, with voluminous sleeves tight at the wrists, and had her gray hair in a large cluster of curls at the temple, the back hair being kept in place by a large tortoiseshell comb similar in shape to the leather withers protector carried on the collar by the horses in a brewer's dray.

There was a pinched, refined air about the aspect of their faces, as if they had led ascetic lives in an aristocratic shade; and as they entered the room side by side, the young ladies approached them, and were received with an old-fashioned courtly grace such as was probably presumed to be correct within these palatial walls.

'Good-morning, aunt dear,' was said to each in turn by the young ladies, in return for which a little birdlike peck of a kiss was given to each soft round face, after which there was silence, each one waiting till there was a scuffle outside, and a little angry muttering, all of which was entirely ignored by the tall, thin, pale ladies, who stood with their mitten-covered hands crossed in front of them, and their eyes cast down.

Everything was so chilly, in spite of its being a warm spring morning, that the advent of a very old and battered but very hot bronze urn seemed quite to send a glow through the room as it was whisked in by the thin young man and placed upon the table, to hurry out and return directly with a crockery toast-rack, full of thin, dry husks of mortified half-burned bread.

Meanwhile, Sister Philippa unlocked a tea-caddy, while Sister Isabella let some hot water run into the pot, and poured it out into the pale blue-and-white cups.

Two caddy-spoonfuls were then placed in the pot, which was duly filled, and Sister Philippa said with grave austereness :

'My dears, will you take your places?'

Then in utter silence the three girls came to the table, and partook with their aunts of the very thin tea, sweetened with no liberal hand, while the bread-and-butter looked untempting and stale.

This went on for some few minutes, every act in connection with the breakfast being performed with scrupulous attention to etiquette, as taught in the highest old-fashioned circles.

'May I give you a little more tea, Clotilde?' 'Will you have the goodness to pass the bread-and-butter,

Marie ?'   'Ruth, I will trouble you, my dear, for the
dry toast.'

After awhile Sister Philippa started an enlivening
conversation on the number of drawing-rooms that
were held by her late Majesty Queen Adelaide at
which they were present as girls, Sister Isabella
being of our opinion that the Court dresses of that
period of history were much more modest, refined
and graceful than those of to-day.

Sister Philippa agreed to this, and with her agree-
ment the breakfast came to an end.

'We will take our morning's walk, my dears, at
once, as it is fine,' said Sister Philippa.   'Will you
go and dress ?'

'Yes, aunt,' was chorused, and the young ladies
rose, curtsied, and retired backwards from the room,
to ascend to their chamber, through which Ruth had
to proceed to get into the cupboard which held her
bed and a small chest of drawers.

The moment they were inside the room, Clotilde
rushed into the middle, gritting her teeth together and
clenching her fists.

'Oh—h—h !' she exclaimed, with a cry of suppressed passion, 'I can't bear it. I shall go mad.'

Then with a bound she dashed to the bed, striking at it and seizing the pillow in her teeth.

Marie got rid of her suppressed vitality by fiercely seizing Ruth by the shoulders, shaking her angrily, and then, as if repenting, catching her about the waist, and waltzing her round the room.

'Oh, Clo! it's horrible,' she cried, loosing Ruth to seize her sister. 'Get up. and let's quarrel or fight, or do something. I can't—I won't—I shan't—I will not bear it. It's like being mummies in a tomb.'

Clotilde turned round, and let herself sink upon the floor, with her head leaning back against the bed, biting the counterpane and twisting it viciously with her hands.

''Rie,' she said at last, and her eyes sparkled as she spoke, 'do you know what happened in the old days to the captive maidens in the stony castles?'

'Yes ; the knights came and rescued them.'

'Then, why don't they come and rescue us? I'll run away with the first man who asks me. I'd marry that thin wretch Joseph to-morrow if he'd have me, and I'd stick pins in him all the rest of his life to see him writhe.'

'I can't bear it much longer,' said Marie, in a low, deep voice; 'I'm nineteen, Clo, and you are turned twenty, and they treat us as if we were little children still. Ah, how I hate them both!'

'Oh, Marie,' said Ruth reproachfully, 'how can you say so!'

'Because I do—I do,' she cried. 'I'm not a soft, smooth thing like you. If this lasts much longer I shall poison them, so as to be hung out of my misery.'

'I shan't,' said Clotilde. 'I say I'll marry the first man who asks me. I will marry him; I'll make him marry me; and then—ah,' she cried fiercely, as she started up, and began pacing up and down, beautiful as some caged leopard, 'once I am free, what I will do! We might as well be nuns.'

'Better,' cried Marie angrily, 'for we should be real prisoners, and expect no better. Now we are supposed to be free.'

'And there'd be some nice fat old father confessors to tease. Better than the smooth-faced, saintly

Paul Montaigne. Oh, how I would confess!' cried Clotilde.

'Old Paul's a prig,' said Marie.

'He's a humbug, I think,' said Clotilde.

'Bother your nice old fat father confessors,' cried Marie, with her eyes gleaming. 'I should like them to be young, and big, and strong, and handsome.'

'And with shaven crowns,' said Clotilde maliciously. 'How should you like them, Ruth?'

'I don't know,' said Ruth simply. 'I have never thought of such a thing.'

'Take that, and that, you wicked story-teller!' cried Clotilde, slapping her arms; 'I know you think more about men than either of us. For my part, the man I mean to have will——'

She stopped, for Marie laid her hand upon her lips, and they both began to prepare themselves for their walk as the grave-looking woman entered the room.

'Oh, you're not ready, then?' she said grimly.

'No, nurse; but we shall be directly.'

'No, you needn't; you're not going.'

'Not going, nurse? Why?'

'The new Lancer regiment is coming to the barracks this morning, and your aunts say some of the officers may be about.'

CHAPTER II.

'WHY didn't I come? Why should I? Very kind
of Lady Millet to ask me, but I'm not a society
man.'

'Oh, but——'

'Yes, I know, lad. Did the affair go off well?'

'Splendidly, only mamma left the wine to the con-
fectioner, and the champagne——'

'Gave you a horrible headache, eh? Serve you
right; should have had toast-and-water.'

'Marcus!'

'So Malpas came, did he?'

'Yes. Bad form, too. I don't like him, Glen.
But that's all over now. Fellow can't always marry
the woman he wants.'

' Can't he ?'

' No, of course not. I wish you had come, though.'

' Thank you ! But you speak in riddles, my little Samson. What's all over now, and what fellow can't always marry the woman he wants ? Speak out, small sage !'

' I say, Glen, I didn't make myself.'

' True, O king !'

' 'Tisn't my fault I'm small.'

' True.'

' You do chaff me so about my size.'

' For the last time : now proceed, and don't lisp and drawl. Who's who ? as Bailey says.'

' I thought I told you before about my sisters ?'

' Often : that you have two pretty sisters—one married and one free.'

' Well, my married sister, Mrs. Morrison, used, I think, to care for Major Malpas.'

' Sorry she had such bad taste.'

This in an undertone.

' Eh ?'

' Go on.'

' Well, it didn't go on or come off, as you call it.'

' As you call it, Dicky.'

' I say, don't talk to me as if I were a bird.'

' All right. Now then, let me finish for you: mamma married the young lady to someone else, and there is just a fag-end of the old penchant left.'

' Oh, hang it, no !'

' I beg pardon !—the young lady's, too. But, my dear Dick, I am one of the most even-tempered of men ; but if you keep up that miserable fashionable drawl and lisp, I shall take hold of you and shake you.'

' But, my dear fellow—weally, Mawcus.'

' Am I to do it ? Say " Marcus" out plain.'

' Mawcus.'

' No ! Marcus.'

' Marcus.'

' That's better. There, hang it all, Dick, you are a soldier ; for heaven's sake be one. Try to be manly, old fellow, and pitch over those silly affectations.'

' It's all very well for you,' said Dick Millet, in an ill-used tone. ' You are naturally manly. Why, you are five feet ten at least, and broad shouldered and strong.'

'While you are only about five feet two, and slight, and have a face as smooth as a girl's.'

'Five feet three and a half,' said the other quickly.

'How do you know?'

'I made the sergeant put me under the standard this morning. I can't help it if I haven't got a heavy brown moustache like you!'

'Who said you could help it, stupid? Why, what a little gander you are, Dick! I'm eight-and-twenty, and you are eighteen.'

'Nineteen!'

'Well, nineteen, then. There, there, you are only a boy yet, so why not be content to be a boy? You'll grow old quite fast enough, my dear lad. Do you know why I like you?'

'Well, not exactly. But you do like me, don't you, Glen?'

'Like you? Yes, when you are what I see before me now, boyish and natural. When you put on those confounded would-be manly airs, and grow affected and mincing as some confounded Burlington Arcade dandy, I think to myself, What a contemptible little puppy it is !'

' I say, you know——' cried the lad, and he tried to look offended.

' Say away, stupid ! Well ?'

Captain Marcus Glen, of Her Majesty's 50th Lancers, a detachment of which, from the head-quarters at Hounslow, were stationed at Hampton Court, sank back in his chair, let fall the newspaper he had been reading, and took out and proceeded to light a cigar, while Richard Millet flushed up angrily, got off the edge of the table where he had been sitting and swinging a neat patent - leather boot adorned with a spur, and seemed for a moment as if he were about to leave the room in a pet.

Marcus Glen saw this and smiled.

' Have a cigar, Dick ?' he said.

The lad frowned, and it was on his lips to say, ' Thanks, I have plenty of my own,' but his eyes met those of the speaker looking kindly and half laugh-ingly in his, and the feeling of reverence for the other's manly attributes, as well as his vanity at being the chosen friend of one he considered to be the finest fellow in the regiment, made him pause, hesitate, and then hold out his hand for the cigar.

'Better not take it, Dick. Tobacco stops the growth.'

The boy paused with the cigar in his hand, and the other burst into a merry laugh, rose lazily, lit a match, and handed it to the young officer, clapping him directly after upon the shoulder.

'Look here, Dick,' he said; 'shall I give you the genuine receipt how to grow into a strong, honest Englishman?'

'Yes,' cried the lad eagerly, the officer and the would-be man dropped, for the school-boy to reassert itself in full force. 'I wish you would, Glen, 'pon my soul I do.'

'Forget yourself then, entirely, and don't set number one up for an idol at whose shrine you are always ready to worship.'

'I don't quite understand you,' said the lad, reddening ingenuously.

'Oh yes, you do, Dick, or you would not have been measured this morning, and made that little nick with the razor on your cheek in shaving off nothing but soap. If you did not worship your con-founded small self, you would not have squeezed your feet into those wretched little boots, nor have waxed those twenty-four hairs upon your upper lip; and 'pon my word, Dick, that really is a work of supererogation, for the world at large, that is to say our little world at large, is perfectly ignorant of their existence.'

'Oh, I say, you are hard on a man, Glen! 'Pon my soul, you are;' and the handsome little fellow looked, with his flushed cheeks and white skin, more girlish than ever.

'Hard? Nonsense! I don't want to see you grow into a puppy. I must give you a lesson now and then, or you'll be spoiled; and then how am I to face Lady Millet after promising what I did?'

'Oh, I had a letter from mamma this morning,' said the lad; 'she sent her kindest regards to you.'

'Thank her for them,' said the young officer. 'Well, so the party went off all right, Dick?'

'Splendid! You ought to have been there. Gertrude would have been delighted to see you.'

'Humph! Out of place, my boy. Lady Millet wants a rich husband for your sister. I'm the wrong colour.'

'Not you. I don't want Gerty to have someone she does not like.'

'But I thought you said that there was a Mr. Huish, or some such name?'

'Well, yes, there is; but it may not come off. Mamma hates the Huishes.'

'You're a character, Dick!' said the officer laughingly. 'There, I'm going to make you dissipated to get you square, so light your cigar, my lad; I won't bully you any more,' he continued, smiling good-humouredly, 'and you may shave till your beard comes if you like, and wax your—your eyebrows—I mean moustache, and dandify yourself a little, for I like to see you smart; but an you love me, as the poet says, no more of that confounded lisp. Now then, you've been reconnoitring, have you, and spying out the barrenness of the land?'

'Yes, and it's a horrible one-eyed sort of a place. Why don't you come and have a look?'

'I shall presently. Seen the Palace?'

'I had a walk round and went into the gardens, which are all very well—old-fashioned, you know; but the private apartments are full of old maids.'

'Ah, yes; maiden ladies and widows. Sort of aristocratic union, I've heard. Good thing for you, Dick.'

'Why?' said the lad, who had again perched himself on the edge of the table and was complacently glancing at his boots.

'Because your inflammable young heart will not be set on fire by antique virgins and blushing widows of sixty.'

'I don't know so much about that,' cried the lad excitedly, taking off his natty little foraging cap. 'Marcus, dear boy, I was walking round a cloister sort of place with a fountain in the middle, and then through a blank square court, and I saw three of the loveliest women, at one of the windows, I ever saw in my life.'

'Distance lends enchantment to the view, my dear boy. If you had gone closer you would have seen the wrinkles and the silvery hairs, if they had not been dyed.'

'I tell you they weren't old,' continued Dick, whose eyes sparkled like those of a girl.

'I'm not a marrying man, for reasons best known to my banker and my creditors.'

'Two of them were dark and the other was fair,' continued the lad, revelling in his description. 'Oh, those two dark girls! You never saw such eyes, such hair, such lovely complexions. Juno-like—that they were. I was quite struck.'

'Foolish?'

'No, no; the Lelys in one of the rooms are nothing to them.'

'Lilies?'

'Nonsense—Lelys: the pictures, Court beauties. I could only stand and gaze at them.'

'Young buck—at gaze,' said the other, smiling at the boy's enthusiasm. 'What was the fair one like?'

'Oh, sweet and Madonnaesque—pensive and gentle. Look here, Marcus, you and I will have a walk round there presently.'

'Not if my name's Marcus,' said the other, laughing. 'Go along, you silly young butterfly, scenting honey in every flower. I say, Dick, shall you go in full review order?'

'I wish you weren't so fond of chaffing a fellow.'

'Did the maidens—old, or young, or doubtful—at the window see our handsome young Adonis with his clustering curls?'

'Hang me if I ever tell you anything again!' cried the lad pettishly. 'Where do you keep your matches? You are always chaffing.'

'Not I,' said the other, turning himself lazily in his chair, 'only I want to see you grow into a matter-of-fact man.'

'Is it a sign of manhood to grow into a Diogenes sort of fellow, who sneers at every woman he sees?' said the lad hotly.

'No, Dick, but it's a sign of hobbledehoyishness to be falling in love with pretty housemaids and boarding-school girls.'

'Which I don't do,' said the lad fiercely.

'Except when you are forming desperate attachments to well-developed ladies, who, after your stupid young heart has been pretty well frizzled in the imaginary fire cast by their eyes, turn out to be other men's wives.'

'I declare you are unbearable, Glen,' cried the lad hotly.

'My dear Dick, you are the most refreshing little chap I ever knew,' said the other, rising. 'There, put on your cap, my boy, and let's go;' and leaving the direction of their course to his younger companion, Captain Glen found himself at last on the broad walk facing the old red-brick Palace.

'I wonder you have never seen it before.'

'So do I; but I never did. Well, old Dutch William had a very good idea of taking care of himself, that's all I can say.'

'But come along here; some of the interior is very curious, especially the quadrangles.'

'So I should suppose,' said Glen drily. 'But I have a fancy for examining some of these quaint old parterres and carven trees, so we'll turn down here.'

Richard Millet's countenance twitched, but he said nothing; and together they strolled about the grounds, the elder pointing out the pretty effects to be seen here and there, the younger seeing nothing but the faces of three ladies standing at a window, and longing to be back in that cloister-like square to gaze upon them again.

'This place will be dull,' said Glen, as he seated himself upon a bench at the edge of a long spread of velvet turf; 'but better than dingy Hounslow, and I've come to the conclusion that we might be much worse off. The society may turn out pretty decent, after all. This old garden will be splendid for a stroll. And—look there, Dick, the inhabitant of the land is fair. Here is another chance for you to fall in love.'

'What, with one of those old——Oh, I say, look, look! I did not see them at first. Those are the very girls.'

For Richard Millet's face had been turned in the other direction, and when he first spoke he had only caught sight of the Honourable Misses Dymcox, walking side by side for their morning walk, closely followed by their three nieces, to make up for a close confinement to the house for three days, consequent upon the coming of the fresh troops to the barracks; the military being a necessary evil in the eyes of these elderly ladies, and such dreadful people that they were to be avoided upon all occasions.

'Oh, those are the damsels, are they?' said Glen, watching the little party as they walked straight on along a broad gravel path. 'The old ladies look as if they were marching a squad of an Amazonian brigade to relieve guard somewhere. My word: how formal and precise! Now, I'll be bound to say, my lad, that you would like to see where they are posted, and go and commit a breach of discipline by talking to the pretty sentries.'

'I should,' cried Dick eagerly. 'Did you notice them?'

'Well, I must own that they are nice-looking, young inflammable, certainly.'

'But that first one, with the dark hair and eyes— she just glanced towards me—isn't she lovely?'

'Well, now, that's odd,' said Glen, smiling. 'I suppose it was my conceit: do you know, I fancied that she glanced at me. At all events, I seemed to catch her eye.'

'Ah, it might seem so, but of course she recognised me again! Let's walk gently after them.'

' What for ?'

' To—er—well, to see which way they go.'

' I don't want to know which way they go, my dear lad, and if I did, why, we can see very well from where we are. There they go, along that path to the right ; you can see their dresses amongst the trees ; and now they have turned off to the left. Would you like to stand upon the seat ?'

' Oh, how cold and impassive you are ! I feel as if I must see which way they go, and then we might take a short cut over the grass, and meet them again.'

' When those two fierce-looking old gorgons would see that you were following them up, and they would fire such a round from their watchful eyes that you, my dear boy, would retire in discomfiture, and looking uncommonly foolish. I remember once, when I was somewhere about your age, I had a very severe encounter with a chaperone in a cashmere shawl.'

' Oh, do get up, Glen, there's a good fellow, and let's go.'

' I had fallen in love with a young lady. I fancy

now that she wore drawers with frills at the bottom, and that her dresses were short—frocks, I believe.'

'There they are again,' cried the boy, jumping up; 'look, they are going down that path.'

'I think the young lady was still in the school-room, but though undeveloped, and given to slipping her shoulders out of the bands of her frock, she was very pretty—bony, but pretty—and I was desperately in love.'

'How wonderfully they are alike in height !'

'I believe,' continued the captain, in a slow, ponderous way, though all the while he seemed to be thoroughly enjoying his companion's eagerness, 'that if I had made love-offerings to my fair young friend—I never knew her name, Dick, and unkindly fate parted us—they would have taken the form of sweet cakes or acidulated drops, and been much appreciated; but alas !——'

'Oh, hang it all, I can't stand this! There goes Malpas. He has seen them, and is making chase. Glen, I shall shoot that fellow, or run him through.'

'What for, my boy ?'

'Because he is always sitting upon me, and making fun of me at the mess. Hang him! I hate him!'

'Don't take any notice of his banter,' said Glen seriously, 'and if he is very unpleasant, it is more dignified to suffer than to fall out. Between ourselves, and in confidence, I advise you not to quarrel with Major Malpas. He can be very disagreeable when he likes.'

'As if I didn't know! He was always hanging after our Renée—Mrs. Frank Morrison, I mean.'

'Indeed!'

'Before she was married, of course.'

'Oh!'

'And used to treat me like a school-boy. I hadn't joined then, you know.'

'No, no, of course not,' said the captain with a peculiar smile.

'But look at him. You can see his black moustache and hooked nose here. He's going straight for them. Look, don't you see?'

'Well, yes, he does seem to be doing as you say. If he is, you may just thank your stars.'

'Thank my stars?   What for?'

'For his getting the snub that you would have received had you been so foolish as to go after those ladies—for they are ladies, Dick.'

'Yes, of course, but it is horrible to be bested like this.   Will you come?'

'No; and I won't let you go.   Sit still, you little stupid, and—there, see how propitious the fates are to you!' he continued, as he saw something unnoticed by his little companion.

'What do you mean?'

'Why, the enemy.'

'The enemy?'

'Well, the Amazonian brigade have seen the demonstration being made by the Major on their left flank, the officer in command has given the order, and they have countermarched and are returning by troops from the left.'

'But are they coming back this way?'

'To be sure they are, and if you sit still you will be able to enfilade them as they retreat.'

'Oh, please don't—pray don't, Glen, there's a good fellow!'

' My dear boy, don't what ?'

' Don't light another cigar. Elderly ladies hate smoking, and you'll send them off in another direction. Besides, it's forbidden.'

' Oh, very well, most inflammable of youths. I shall have to make this the subject of a despatch to mamma.'

' Hush ! be quiet. Don't seem to notice them, or they may turn off another way. I say, old Malpas is done.'

' And you are able to deliver a charge without change of position.'

It might have been from design, or it might have been pure accident, for ladies' pockets always do seem made to hold their contents unsafely. Certain it was, however, that as the Honourable Misses Dymcox marched stiffly by, closely followed by their nieces, all looking straight before them, and as if they were not enjoying their walk in the slightest degree, there was a glint of something white, and Clotilde's little old and not particularly fine hand-kerchief fell to the ground.

Glen saw it, and did not move.

Richard Millet did not see it for the moment, but as soon as it caught his eye he impulsively dashed from his seat, picked it up, and ran a few steps after the little party.

' Excuse me,' he exclaimed.

' Oh, thank you,' said Clotilde ; and she stretched out her hand to take the handkerchief, but in a quick, unobtrusive way Miss Isabella interposed her thin stiff form, received the handkerchief from the young officer with a formal obeisance, and before he could recover from the paralyzing chill of her severe look, the party had passed on.

' But I had a good look at her,' he cried excitedly, as he rejoined his companion.

' And that severe lady had a good look at you, Dick. What a cold, steely glance it was !'

' But did you see her eyes, Glen—dark as night !' he cried rapturously. ' Did you see the glance *she* gave me ?'

' No,' said the young officer bluntly, ' seemed to me as if she wanted her glasses ;' and then to himself, ' She is handsome, and if it were not conceited, I should say she was looking at me.'

CHAPTER III.

PLUMP, blonde Lady Millet uttered an ejaculation and made a gesture of annoyance as she settled herself in a luxurious lounge.

'Now, do for goodness' sake wipe your eyes, Gertrude, and be sensible if you can! I declare it's enough to worry one to death. Once for all, I tell you I do not like these Huishes, and what your father could have been about to listen to your uncle Robert and bring that young man here I can't think.'

Gertrude Millet forced back her tears, and bent lower over some work upon which she was engaged in the drawing-room of her father's house in Grosvenor Square.

'They are very plebeian sort of people, and they have no money; but because his father was an old friend of your uncle Robert's when he was a young man, this Mr. John Huish must be invited here, and you, you silly child! must let him make eyes at you.'

'Really, mamma——'

'Now do let me speak, Gertrude,' said Lady Millet severely. 'It is as I say, and I will not have it. Sentimentality does very well for low-class people, but we have a position to maintain, and I have other views for you.'

'But, mamma, you never thought Frank Morrison plebeian,' said Gertrude, raising her bright gray eyes to bring them to bear on her dignified mother, who was arranging the lace about her plump white throat.

'My dear child, comparisons are odious, and at your age you should allow people to think for you. Does it ever occur to you that your mother's sole wish—the object for which she almost entirely lives—is to see her child happily settled in life? No, no; don't speak, please: you hurt me. I consented to your sister Renée's union with Frank for many reasons. Certainly his family is plebeian, but he is a young man whom I am rejoiced to see determined to make use of his wealth to his own elevation—to marry well, and be the founder of a new family of gentry.'

'But I'm sure Renée is not happy, mamma.'

'Then, in her position, it is her own fault, my dear, of course. I had been married years before I had a second carriage. Once for all, there is no comparison between Frank and this Mr. Huish. If it had not been out of commiseration for your uncle Robert —it being his wish—Mr. Huish would not have been received here at all.'

Gertrude bit her nether lip, and bent lower over her work as sweet and lovable a face as girl of twenty could have.

'Your uncle is a most unhappy man; and if he were not so rich people would call him insane, living such an absurd life as he does. I often feel as if I must go and rouse him up, and force him to act like a Christian. By the way, you have not been to see him lately?'

'No, mamma.'

'Call, then, soon. He must not be neglected. We have our duties to do, and that is one of them. He is always kind to you?'

'Always, mamma.'

'That is right. You must humour him, for he seems to have taken a most unnatural dislike to Richard.'

'Yes, mamma.'

'Do you think so?' said Lady Millet sharply.

'He forbade Dick to call again after he had importuned him for money.'

'Foolish, reckless boy! That's the way young people always seem to me determined to wreck their prospects. Your uncle Robert has no one else to leave his money to but you children, and yet you persist in running counter to his wishes.'

'I, mamma?'

'All of you. Do you suppose because he desired your father to take a little more notice of this John Huish that you were to throw yourself at his head?'

Gertrude squeezed her eyelids very tightly together, and took three or four stitches in the dark.

'I have always found Uncle Robert particularly kind to me.'

'And so he would be to Renée and to Richard if they were not so foolish. I declare I don't know what that boy can possibly do with his money. But, there, I suppose being in a regiment is expensive.'

'Do you like Major Malpas, mamma?' said Gertrude suddenly.

'Certainly not!' said Lady Millet tartly; 'and really, Gertrude, you are a most extraordinary girl! John Huish one moment, Major Malpas the next. Huish was bad enough; now don't, for goodness' sake, go throwing yourself at Major Malpas.'

'Mamma!'

'Will you let me speak, child?' cried Lady Millet angrily. 'I don't know what you girls are thinking about! Why, you are as bad as Renée! If I had not been firm, she would have certainly accepted him, and he is a man of most expensive habits. It was most absurd of Renée. But there: that's over. But I do rather wonder at Frank making so much of a friend of him. Oh dear me, no, Gertrude! that would be impossible!'

'Of course, mamma!'

'Then why did you talk in that tone?'

'Because I don't like Major Malpas, and I am sure Renée does not, either.'

'Of course she does not. She is a married lady. Surely she can be civil to people without always thinking of liking! It was a curious chance that Richard should be gazetted into the same regiment; and under the circumstances I have been bound to invite him and that other officer, Captain Glen, here, for they can help your brother, no doubt, a great deal. You see, I have to think of everything, for your poor father only thinks now of his dinners and his clubs.'

Gertrude sighed and went on with her work, while Lady Millet yawned, got up, looked out of the window, and came back.

'Quite time the carriage was round. Then I am to go alone?'

'I promised Renée to be in this morning,' said Gertrude quietly.

'Ah, well; then I suppose you must stop. I wonder whether Lady Littletown will take any notice of Richard now he is at Hampton Court?'

'I should think she would, mamma. She is always most friendly.'

'Friendly, but not trustworthy, my dear. A terribly scheming woman, Gertrude. Her sole idea seems to be match-making. But, there, Richard is too young to become her prey!'

Gertrude's brow wrinkled, and she looked wonderingly at her mother, whose face was averted.

'I have been looking up the Glens. Not a bad family, but a younger branch. I suppose Richard will accompany his brother officer here one of these days. By the way, my dear, Lord Henry Moorpark seemed rather attentive to you at the Lindleys the other night.'

'Yes, mamma,' said Gertrude quietly; 'he took me in to supper, and sat and chatted with me a long time.'

'Yes; I noticed that he did.'

'I like Lord Henry, mamma; he is so kind and gentle and courteous.'

'Very, my dear.'

'One always feels as if one could confide in him— he is so fatherly, and——'

My dear Gertrude!'

'What have I said, mamma?'

'Something absurd. Fatherly! What nonsense! Lord Henry is in the prime of life, and you must not talk like that. You girls are so foolish! You think of no one but boys with pink and white faces and nothing to say for themselves. Lord Henry Moorpark is a most *distingué* gentle—I mean a nobleman; and judging from the attentions he began to pay you the other night, I——'

'Oh, mamma! surely you cannot think that?'

'And pray why not, Gertrude?' said Lady Millet austerely. 'Why should not I think *that?* Do you suppose I wish to see my youngest daughter marry some penniless boy? Do, pray, for goodness' sake, throw away all that bread-and-butter, school-girl, sentimental nonsense. It is quite on the cards that Lord Henry Moorpark may propose for you.'

'Oh dear,' thought Gertrude; 'and I was talking to him so warmly about John Huish!'

Gertrude's red lips parted, showing her white teeth, and the peachy pink faded out of her cheeks as she sat there with her face contracting, and a cloud seemed to come over her young life, in whose shadow she saw herself, and her future as joyless as that of the sister who had been married about a year earlier to a wealthy young north Yorkshire manufacturer, who was now neglecting her and making her look old before her time.

'There, it must be nearly three,' said Lady Millet, rising; 'I'll go and put on my things. I shall not come in again, Gertrude. Give my love to Renée, and if Lord Henry Moorpark does come—but, there, I have perfect faith in your behaving like a sensible girl. By the way, Richard may run up. If he does, try and keep him to dinner. I don't half like his being at that wretched Hampton Court; it is so terribly suggestive of holiday people and those dread-ful vans.'

With these words Lady Millet sailed out of the room, thinking to herself that a better managing mother never lived, and a quarter of an hour after she entered her carriage to go and distribute cards at the houses of her dearest friends.

CHAPTER IV.

THE REMAINS OF A FALL.

GERTRUDE MILLET'S anxious look grew deeper as she sat with her work in her lap, thinking of John Huish and certain tender passages which had somehow passed between them ; then of Lord Henry Moorpark, the pleasant, elderly nobleman whose attentions had been so pleasant and so innocently received ; and as she thought of him a burning blush suffused her cheeks, and she tried to recall the words he had last spoken to her.

The consequence was a fit of low spirits, which did not become high when later on Mrs. Frank Morrison called, dismissed her carriage, and sat chatting for some time with her sister, Lady Millet being, she said, in the park.

'You need not tell me I look well,' said Gertrude, pouting slightly. 'I declare you look miserable.'

'Oh no, dear, only a little low-spirited to-day. Have you called on Uncle Robert lately?'

'Without you? No.'

'Then let's go.'

Gertrude jumped at the suggestion, and half an hour later the sisters were making their way along Wimpole Street the gloomy, to stop at last before the most wan-looking of all the dreary houses in that most dreary street. It was a house before which no organ-man ever stopped to play, no street vendor to shout his wares, nor passer-by to examine from top to bottom; the yellow shutters were closed, and the appearance of the place said distinctly 'out of town.' The windows were very dirty, but that is rather a fashion in Wimpole Street, where the windows get very dirty in a month, very much dirtier in two months, and as dirty as possible in three. They, of course, never get any worse, for when once they have arrived a this pitch they may go for years, the weather rather improving them, what with the rain's washing and the sun's bleaching.

The paint of the front door was the worst part about that house, for the sun had raised it in little blisters, which street boys could not bear to see without cracking and picking off in flakes ; and the consequence was that the door looked as if it had had a bad attack of some skin disease, and a new cuticle of a paler hue was growing beneath the old.

Wimpole Street was then famous for the knockers upon its doors. They were large and resounding. In fact, a clever manipulator could raise a noise that would go rolling on a still night from nearly one end of the street to the other. For, in their wisdom, our ancestors seized the idea of a knocker on that sounding-board, a front door, as a means to warn servants downstairs that someone was waiting, by a deafening noise that appealed to those in quite a different part of the place. But this was not allowed at the house with the blistered front door, for a great staple had been placed over one side for years, and when you had passed the two great iron extinguishers that were never used for links, and under the fantastic ironwork that had never held a lamp since the street had been lit with gas, and, ascending

three steps, stood at the door, you could only contrive
quite a diminutive kind of knock, such as was given
upon that occasion by Renée, for Gertrude was carrying a large bouquet of flowers.

The knock was hard enough to bring a little
bleached, sparrow-like man, dressed in black, to the
door, and his colourless face, made more pallid by
a little black silk cap he wore, brightened as he held
his head first on one side, then on the other, his
triangular nose adding to his sparrow-like appearance, and giving a stranger the idea that he would
never kiss anyone, but would peck.

'How is my uncle this morning, Vidler?' said
Gertrude.

'Capital, miss,' said the little man, holding wide
the door for the ladies to enter, and closing it quickly,
lest, apparently, too much light should enter at the
same time.

For the place was very gloomy and subdued within. The great leather porter's chair, the umbrella-
stand, and the pictures all looked sombre and black.
Even the two classical figures holding lamps, that had
not been lighted for a quarter of a century at least,

were swarthy, and a stranger would have gone stumbling and feeling his way along ; but not so Vidler, Captain Robert Millet's handy servant. He was as much at home in the gloom as an owl, and in a quick, hurried way that was almost spasmodic he led the visitors upstairs, but only to stop on the first landing.

'If I might make so bold, Miss Gertrude,' he said, holding his head on one side. 'I don't often see a flower now.'

The girl held up the bouquet, and the little man had a long sniff with a noise as if taking a pinch of snuff, said, 'Thank you, miss,' and went on up to the back drawing-room door, which was a little lighter than the staircase, for the top of the shutters of one of the three tall narrow windows was open.

A glance round the room showed that it was scrupulously clean. Time had blackened the paint and ceiling, but everything that could be cleaned or polished was in the highest state of perfection.

For Valentine Vidler and his wife Salome, being very religious and conscientious people, told themselves and one another nearly every day that as the master never supervised anything it was the more their duty to keep the place in the best of order. For instance, Vidler would say :

'I don't think I shall clean all that plate over this week, Salome. It's as bright as it can be.'

When to him Salome: 'Valentine, there's One above who knows all, and though your master may not know that you have not cleaned the plate, He will.'

'That's very true, Salome,' the little man would say with a sigh, and then set to work in a green baize apron, and was soon be-rouged up to the eyes as he polished away.

Another day, perhaps, it would be Salome's turn ; for the temptation, as she called it, would attack her. The weather would be hot, perhaps, and a certain languid feeling, the result of a want of change, would come over her.

'Valentine,' she would say, perhaps, 'I think the big looking-glass in the drawing-room will do this week ; it's as clean as clean.'

'Hah!' would say Valentine, with a sigh, 'Satan has got tight hold of you again, my dear little woman. It is your weakness that you ought to resist. Do you think the Lord cannot see those three fly-specks at the bottom corner? Resist the temptation, woman ; resist it.'

Then little Salome, who was a tiny plump downy woman, who somehow reminded people of a thick potato-shoot that had grown in the dark, would sigh, put on an apron that covered her all over except her face, climb on a pair of steps, and polish the great mirror till it was as clear as hands could make it.

She was a pleasant-faced little body, and very neatly dressed. There was a little fair sausage made up of rolled-up hair on each side of her face, two very shiny smooth surfaces of hair over her forehead, and a neat little white line up the centre, the whole being surmounted by one of those quaint high-crowned caps which project over to the front. In fact, there was, in spite of the potato-shoot allusion, a good deal of resemblance in little Mrs. Vidler to a plump charity child, especially as she wore an apron with a bib, a white muslin kerchief crossed over her bosom, and a pair of muslin sleeves up to her elbows.

The little woman was in the drawing-room armed with a duster as Valentine showed up the young

ladies, and she faced round and made two little bobs,
quite in the charity-school-child fashion, as taught by
those who so carefully make it the first duty of such
children to obey their pastors and masters, and order
themselves lowly and reverently, and make bobs and
bows to—all their betters.

'Why, my dears, I am glad you're come,' she
exclaimed. 'Miss Renée—there, I beg your pardon
—Mrs. Morrison, what an age it is since I saw you!
And only to think you are a married lady now, when
only the other day you two were little things, and I
used to bring you one in each hand, looking quite
frightened, into this room

'Ah yes, Salome, times are changed,' said Renée
sadly. 'How is uncle?'

'Very well, my dear,' said the little woman, holding
her head on one side to listen in the same bird-like
way adopted by her husband. 'He's not in his room
yet. But what beautiful flowers!'

She, too, inhaled the scent precisely in her husband's fashion, before fetching a china bowl from a
chiffonier, and carefully wiping it inside and out,
though it was already the perfection of cleanliness.

'A jug of clean water, if you please, Vidler,' she
said softly.

'Yes, my dear,' said the little man, smiling at the
sisters, and giving his hands a rub together, before
obeying his wife.

'I was so sorry, Miss Renée—there, I must call
you so, my dear; it's so natural—I was so sorry that
I did not see you when you came. Only to think of
my being out a whole month nursing my poor sister!
I hadn't been away from the place before for twenty
years, and poor Vidler was so upset without me.
And I don't think,' she added, nodding, 'that master
liked it.'

'I'm sure he would not,' said Gertrude; and then,
the little man coming in very quietly and closing the
door after him, water was poured in the china bowl,
the flowers duly deposited therein and placed upon a
small mahogany bracket in front of a panel in the
centre of the room.

'There, my dears, I'll go now. I dare say he will
not be long.'

The little woman smiled at the sisters, and the
little man nodded at them in a satisfied way as if he

thought them very pleasant to look upon. Then, taking his wife's hand, they toddled together out of the room.

A quaint, subdued old room—clean, and yet comfortless. Upon a wet day, when a London fog hung over the streets and filled the back yards, no female could have sat in it for an hour without moistening her handkerchief with tears. For it was, in its dim twilight, like a drawing-room of the past, full of sad old memories of the dead and gone, who haunted it and clung to its furniture and chairs. It was impossible to sit there long without peopling the seats with those who once occupied them—without seeing soft, sad faces reflected in the mirrors, or hearing fancied footsteps on the faded carpet.

And it was so now, as the sisters sat thinking in silence, Renée with her head resting upon her hand, Gertrude with her eyes closed, half dreaming of what might have been.

For Gertrude's thoughts ran back to a miniature in her father's desk of a handsome, sun-browned young man in uniform, bright-eyed, keen, and animated; and she thought of what she had heard of his history: how he had loved some fair young girl before his regiment was ordered away to Canada. How he had come back to find that she had become another's, and then that some terrible struggle had occurred between him and his rival, and the young officer had been maimed for life—turned in one minute from the strong, vigorous man to a misanthrope, who dragged himself about with difficulty, half paralyzed in his lower limbs, but bruised more painfully in his heart. For, broken in spirit as in body, he had shut himself up, after his long illness, never seeing a soul, never going out of the closely shuttered rooms that he had chosen for himself in his lonely faded house.

Vidler had been a drummer in his regiment, she had heard, and he had devoted himself to the master who had fetched him in when lying wounded under fire ; and in due time Vidler had married and brought his little wife to the house, the couple never leaving it except on some emergency, but growing to like the darkness in which they dwelt, and sternly doing their duty by him they served.

' Poor uncle !' sighed Gertrude, as she thought of his

desolate life, and her own sad position. ' I wonder who it was he loved.'

As the thought crossed her mind, there was a slight noise in the next room, like the tapping of a stick upon the floor, and Gertrude laid her hand upon her sister's arm.

Then the noise ceased, and the little panel, about a foot square, before which the flowers had been placed, was drawn aside, seeming to run into a groove.

The sisters did not move, but waited, knowing from old experience that at a word or movement on their part the panel would be clapped impatiently to, and that their visit would be a fruitless one.

A stranger would have thought of rats and the action of one of those rodents in what took place ; for now that the panel had been slid back, all remained perfectly still, as if the mover were listening and watching. Then at last a thin, very white hand appeared, lifted the flowers out of the bowl, and they disappeared.

There was not even a rustling noise heard for a few minutes, during which the sisters sat patiently waiting.

At last there was a faint sigh ; and a cold—so to speak, colourless—voice said :

'Is Gertrude there ?'

'Yes, dear uncle,' said the young girl eagerly.

'Anyone else ?'

'I am here too, dear uncle,' said Renée.

'Hah ! I am glad to hear you, my children—glad to hear you.   How is my brother ?'

'Papa is not very well, uncle,' said Gertrude. 'Poor dear, his cough is very troublesome.'

'Poor Humphrey ! he is so weak,' said the voice, in the same cold, monotonous way that was almost repulsive in its chilling tone.   'Tell him, when he is well enough, he can come and talk to me for half an hour.   I cannot bear more.'

'Yes, dear uncle, I will tell him,' said Renée.

Then there was another pause, and at last the thin white hand stole cautiously forth, half covered with a lace frill, and the cold voice said :

'Renée !'

The young wife left her seat, went forward, took it in her ungloved hand, and kissed it.   Then she returned to her place, and the voice said :

'Gertrude!'

The young girl went through the same performance, and as she loosed it, the hand was passed gently over both her cheeks, and then withdrawn, when Gertrude returned to her seat, and there was again silence.

'You are not happy, Renée,' said the voice at last, in its cold measured accents; 'there was a tear on my hand.'

Renée sighed, but made no reply.

'Gertrude, child, I like duty towards parents; but I think a daughter goes too far when, at their wish, she marries a man she does not love.'

'Oh, uncle dear,' cried Gertrude hysterically, 'pray, pray, do not talk like this!'

She made a brave effort to keep back her tears, and partially succeeded, for Renée softly knelt down by her side and drew her head close to her breast.

'Poor children!' said the voice again. 'I am sorry, but I cannot help you. You must help yourselves.'

There was a nervous, querulous tone in the voice now, as if the suppressed sobs that faintly rose troubled the speaker, but it had passed when the voice was heard once more in a quiet way, more like an appeal than a command :

'Sing to me.'

The sisters rose and went to a very old-fashioned grand piano, opened it, and Gertrude's fingers swept the wiry jangling chords which sounded quite in keeping with the room ; then, subduing the music as much as possible, so that their fresh young voices dominated, rising and falling in a rich harmony that floated through the room, they sang the old, old duet, 'Flow on, thou shining river.' Every note seemed to have in it the sadness of age, the mournful blending of the bygone when hope was young and disappointment and care had not crushed with a load of misery a heart once fresh as those of the singers.

A deep sigh came from the little panel, unheard, though, by the two girls, and the hand appeared once more for the thin white fingers to tap the wood gently in unison with the music, which was inexpressibly sweet, though sad.

For how is it that those melodies of the past, even though major, seemed to acquire a mournful tone that is not minor, but has all its sad sweetness? Take what pathetic air you will of a generation or two back, and see if it has not acquired within your knowledge a power of drawing tears that it had not in the days of old.

From the simple duet, first one and then the other glided to the old-fashioned ditties popular thirty or forty years before. 'Those evening bells,' 'Waters of Elle,' and the like, till, without thinking, Gertrude began 'Love not,' her sweet young voice sounding intensely pathetic as she went on, gradually gathering inspiration from the words, till in the midst of the sweetest, most appealing strain, she uttered a cry of misery, and threw herself sobbing into her sister's arms.

'Oh, Gerty, darling, why did you sing that?' whispered Renée, trying to soothe her, as her own tears fell fast, but for a few minutes in vain, till by a brave effort Gertrude got the better of her hysterical feelings, and, hastily wiping her eyes, glanced towards the panel, where the bowl of water stood upon the bracket, but the opening was closed.

The sisters looked piteously at one another, and Renée whispered:

'Speak to him. Tell him you did not wish to make him angry.'

Gertrude glided to the panel, and, stifling a sob, she said softly:

'Uncle, dear uncle, do not be cross with me—I am very sorry. I was so miserable.'

There was no reply—no sound to indicate that the words had been heard; and after waiting for about a quarter of an hour the two girls crossed to the door, went slowly out, and found that they had had an audience in the shape of Valentine Vidler and his wife, who had been seated upon the stairs.

'Thank you, my dears,' said Salome, nodding and smiling. 'We like to hear you sing. You have made a very long stay to-day, and his lunch is quite ready.'

The sisters were too heartsore to trust themselves to say much, and Vidler opened the door for them, admitting as little light as he could by closing it directly and going to assist his wife.

'Renée,' said Gertrude as they reached the square, 'do you remember what Uncle Robert said?'

'Yes. He could not help us—we must help ourselves.'

'Then——' There was a pause.

'Yes, dear, what?'

'I'm sure mamma is planning for me to marry Lord Henry Moorpark.'

'I'm afraid so.'

'And I'm sure, Ren dear, he's a dear, amiable, nice old man; but if he proposes I never will say "Yes."'

There was another pause, and then Renée smiled, passed her arm round her handsome sister's neck, and kissed her lovingly.

'Have you got John Huish very bad?' she whispered.

Gertrude's cheeks were crimson, and the colour flushed into her neck as she flung her arms round her sister and hid her face on her breast.

CHAPTER V.

DR. STONOR'S PATIENT.

'THE doctor at home?'

This to a quiet, sedate-looking man in livery, who opened the door of one of the serious-looking houses in Finsbury Circus, where, upon a very shiny brass plate, were in Roman letters the words 'Dr. Stonor.'

There was not much in those few black letters, but many a visitor had gone up the carefully-whitened steps, gazed at them, stepped down again with a curious palpitation of the heart, and walked right round the Circus two or three times to gain composure enough before once more ascending the steps and knocking at the door.

There had been cases—not a few—where visitors had spent weeks in making up their minds to go to

Dr. Stonor, and had reached his doorstep only to hurry back home quite unable to face him, and then suffer in secret perhaps for months to come.

For what would that interview reveal? That the peculiar sensations or pains were due to some trifling disorganization that a guinea and a prescription would set right, or that the seeds of some fatal disease had begun to shoot?

Daniel, factotum to Dr. Stonor, had been standing like a spider watching at the slip of a window beside the door waiting for sick flies to come into the doctor's net.

'Old game!' said Daniel to himself, as he drew back from the window to observe unseen, and without moving a muscle in his face. For it was Daniel's peculiarity that he never did move the muscles of his face. He would hold a patient for his master during a painful operation, be scolded, badgered, see harrowing scenes, receive vails, hear praise or abuse of the doctor—for these are both applied to medicine men— and all without making a sign, losing his nerve, or being elated. Daniel was always the same—clean, quiet, self-possessed; and he had seen handsome

fair-bearded John Huish descend from a cab, walk up
to the door, pass by and go slowly and thoughtfully
on, passing his hand over his thick golden beard,
looking very tall, manly, and unpatientlike, as he
passed on round the Circus.

'He'll be back in ten minutes,' said Daniel to
himself, as he admitted a regular patient and once
more closed the door. It was a quarter of an hour,
though, before John Huish came to the house, asked
if the doctor was at home, was shown into the
waiting-room, and in due course came face to face
with the keen, gray, big-headed, clever-looking little
practitioner.

'Ah, Huish, my dear boy! Glad to see you, John.
Sit down. This is kind of you, to look me up. I've
only just come back from a fishing trip—trouting.
Old habit. Down this way?'

'Well, no, doctor,' said the young man hesitatingly.
'The fact is, I came to consult you.'

'Glad of it. I was the first person who ever took
hold of your little hand, and the tiny fingers clutched
one of mine as if you trusted me. And you always
kept it up—eh? I'm very glad.'

'Glad, sir ?'

'Of course I am,' said the doctor, taking out his
keys and unlocking a drawer. 'What is it, my boy
—a little cheque ?'

'Oh dear no, doctor.'

'Nothing serious, I hope.'

'I hope not. I thought I would consult you.'

'That's right, my lad. Well, what is it? Going
to buy a horse—speculate in the funds—try a yachting trip ?'

'My dear sir,' said Huish, smiling, 'you do not
understand me. I am afraid I am ill.'

'Ill? You? Ill?' said the doctor, jumping up
and laying his hands on the young man's shoulders
as he gazed into his frank, earnest eyes. 'Get
up, Jack. You were almost my first baby, and I was
very proud of you. Finest built little fellow I ever
saw. There, put out your tongue'—he was obeyed
—'let's feel your pulse'—this was done—'here, let
me listen at your chest. Pull a long, deep breath ;'
and the doctor listened, made him pull off his coat
and clapped his ear to his back, rumpled his shirt-front
as he tapped and punched him all over, concluding by

giving the visitor a back-handed slap in the chest, and resuming his seat, exclaiming :

'Why, you young humbug, what do you mean by coming here with such a cock-and-bull story? Your physique is perfect. You are as sound as a bell. You are somewhere about thirty years old, and you are a deuced good-looking young fellow. What do you want?'

'You take my breath away, doctor,' said the young man, smiling. 'I want to explain.'

'Explain away, then, my dear boy; but, for goodness' sake, don't be such an ass as to think the first time you are a bit bilious, or hipped, or melancholy, that you are ill. Oh, by the way, while I think of it, I had a letter from your people yesterday. They want me to have a run down to Shropshire.'

'Why not go?'

'Again? I can't. Fifty people want me, and they would swear to a man if I went away that I was indirectly murdering them. But come, I keep on chattering. Now then, I say, what's the matter? In love?'

The colour deepened a little on the white forehead, and the visitor replied quietly :

'I should not consult a physician for that ailment. The fact is, that for some while past I have felt as if my memory were going.'

'Tut ! nonsense !'

'At times it seems as if a perfect cloud were drawn between the present and the past. I can't account for it—I do not understand it; but things I have done one week are totally forgotten by me the next.'

'If they are bad things, so much the better.'

'You treat it very lightly, sir, but it troubles me a great deal.'

'My dear boy, I would not treat it lightly if I thought there was anything in it; but you do not and never have displayed a symptom of brain disease, neither have your father and mother before you. You are not dissipated.'

'Oh no ! I never——'

'You may spare yourself the trouble of talking, John, my boy. I could tell in a moment if you had a bit of vice in you, and I know you have not. But come, my lad : to be serious, what has put this crotchet into your head ?'

'Crotchet or no,' said the young man sadly, 'I have for months past been tormented with fears that I have something wrong in the head—incipient insanity, or idiocy, if you like to call it so.'

'I don't like to call it anything of the kind, John Huish,' said the doctor tartly, 'because it's all non-sense. I have not studied insanity for the last five-and-twenty years without knowing something about it; so you may dismiss that idea from your mind. But come, let's know something more about this terrible bugbear.'

'Bugbear if you like, doctor, but here is the case. Every now and then I have people—friends, ac-quaintances—reminding me of things I have pro-mised—engagements I have made—and which I have not kept.'

'What sort of engagements ?' said the doctor.

'Well, generally about little bets, or games at cards.'

'That you owe money on ?'

'Yes,' said Huish eagerly. 'I have again and again been asked for money that I owe.'

' Or are said to owe,' said the doctor drily.

' Oh, there is no doubt about it,' said Huish.
' About a twelvemonth ago, when this sort of thing
began——'

' What sort of thing?' said the doctor.

' These lapses of memory,' replied Huish.

' Oh !'

' I used to be annoyed, and denied them, till I began
to be scouted by the men I knew; and at last one
or two of them brought unimpeachable witnesses to
prove that I was in the wrong.'

' Oh, John Huish, my dear boy, how can you let
yourself be imposed upon so easily !'

' There is no imposition, I assure you. I give you
the facts.'

' Facts ! Did you ever know anyone come and tell
you that he owed you money, and pay you?'

' Yes, half a dozen times over—heavier amounts
than I have had to pay.'

' Humph ! that's strange,' said the doctor, looking
curiously at his visitor.

' Strange?—it's fearful !' cried the young man
passionately. ' It is getting to be a curse to me,

and I cannot shake off the horrible feeling that I am losing my mind—that I am going wrong. And if this be the case, I cannot bear it, especially just now, when——'

He checked himself, and gazed piteously at the man to whom he had come for help.

'Be cool, boy. Supposing it is as you say, it is only a trifle, perhaps; but it seems to me that there is a great deal of imagination in it.'

'Oh no—oh no! I fear I am going, slowly but surely, out of my mind.'

'Because you forget things after a certain time, eh? Stuff! Don't be foolish. Why, you never used to think that your brain was going wrong when you were a schoolboy, and every word of the lesson that you knew perfectly and said *verbatim* to a school-fellow dropped out of your mind.'

'No.'

'Of course you did not; and as to going mad, why, my dear boy, have you any idea what a lunatic is?'

'I cannot say that I have.'

'Well, then, you shall have,' said the doctor; 'and that will do you more good than all my talking. You shall see for yourself what a diseased mind really is, and that will strengthen you mentally, and show you how ill-advised are your fancies.'

'But, doctor, I should not like to be a witness of the sufferings of others.'

'Nonsense, my boy. There, pray don't imagine, because I live at Highgate, and am licensed to have so many insane patients under my care, that you are going to see horrible creatures dressed in straw and grovelling in cells. My dear John, I am going to ask you to a mad dinner-party.'

'A mad dinner-party?'

'Well, there, to come and dine with my sister, myself, and our patients. No people hung in chains or straw. Perfectly quiet gentlemen, my dear fellow, but each troubled with a craze. You would not know that they had anything wrong if they did not break out now and then upon the particular subject. Come to-night at seven sharp.'

The doctor glanced at his watch, rose, and held out his hand ; and though John Huish hesitated, the doctor's eyes seemed to force him to say that he would be there, and he began to feel for his purse.

'Look here, sir,' said the doctor, stopping him : 'if you are feeling for fees, don't insult your father's old friend by trying to offer him one. There, till seven —say half-past six—and I'll give you a glass of burgundy, my boy, that shall make you forget all these imaginations.'

'Thank you, doctor——'

'Not another word, sir, but *au revoir.*'

'*Au revoir,*' said Huish ; and he was shown out, to go back to his chambers thinking about his ailment —and Gertrude, while the doctor began to muse.

'Strange that I should take so much interest in that boy. Heigho! Some years now since I went fly-fishing, and fished his father out of the pit.'

CHAPTER VI.

AUNT PHILIPPA ON MATRIMONY.

' WILL you speak, Isabella, or shall I ?'

'If you please, Philippa, will you ?' said her sister with frigid politeness.

The Honourable Miss Dymcox motioned to her nieces to seat themselves, and they sat down.

Then there was a sharp premonitory 'Hem !' and a long pause, during which the thoughts of the young ladies went astray.

'I wonder what that officer's name is,' thought Clotilde, 'and whether that good-looking boy is his squire ?'

Rather a romantic notion this, by the way, and it gave Marcus Glen in the young lady's ideas the

position of knight; but it was excusable, for her life
had been secluded in the extreme.

'What a very handsome man that dark officer was
that we nearly met! but I don't like his looks,' mused
Marie ; and then, as Ruth was thinking that she would
rather be getting on with some of the needlework that
fell to her share than listening to her aunt's lecture—
one of the periodical discourses it was their fate to
hear—there was another sharp 'Hem !'

'Marriage,' said the Honourable Miss Dymcox, 'is
an institution that has existed from the earliest ages
of the world.'

Had a bomb-shell suddenly fallen into the chilly,
meanly-furnished drawing-room, where every second
article seemed to wear a brown-holland pinafore, and
the frame of the old-fashioned mirror was tightly
draped in yellow canvas, the young ladies could not
have looked more astonished.

In their virgin innocency the word 'marriage' had
been tabooed to them, and consequently was never
mentioned, being a subject held to be unholy for the
young people's ears.

Certainly there were times when the wedding of

some lady they knew was canvassed; but it was with extreme delicacy, and not in the downright fashion of Miss Philippa's present speech.

'Ages of the world,' assented the Honourable Isabella, opening a pale drab fan, and using it gently, as if the subject made her warm.

'And,' continued Miss Philippa, 'I think it right to speak to you children, now that you are verging upon womanhood, because it is possible that some day or another you might either of you receive a proposal.'

'That sun-browned officer with the heavy moustache,' thought Clotilde, whose cheeks began to glow. 'She thinks he may try to be introduced. Oh, I wish he may!'

'When your poor—I say it with tears, Isabella.'

'Yes, sister, with tears,' assented that lady.

'I am addressing you, Clotilde and Marie,' continued Miss Philippa. 'You, Ruth, of course cannot be answerable for the stroke of fate which placed you in our hands, an adopted child.'

'An adopted child,' said Miss Isabella, closing her fan, for the moral atmosphere seemed cooler.

'When your poor mother, your poor, weak mamma,

children, wantonly and recklessly, and in opposition
to the wishes of all her relatives, insisted upon marrying Mr. Julian Riversley, who was never even acknowledged by any member of our family——'

'I remember papa as being very handsome, and
with dark hair,' said Marie.

'Marie!' exclaimed the Honourable Misses Dymcox
in a breath.   'I am surprised at you!'

'Pray be silent, child,' added Miss Philippa.

'Yes, aunt.'

'I say your poor mamma must have known that
she was degrading the whole family—degrading us,
Isabella.'

'Yes, sister, degrading us,' assented that lady.

'By marrying a penniless man of absolutely no
birth.'

'Whatever,' assented Miss Isabella.

'As I have often told you, children, it was during
the corrupting times of the Commonwealth that the
lineal descendants of Sir Guy Dymcoques—the *s* not
sounded, my dears—allowed the family name to be
altered into Dymcox, which by letters patent was
made imperative, and the proper patronymic has

never been restored to its primitive orthography. It is a blot on our family history to which I will no more allude.'

Miss Isabella allowed the fan to fall into her lap, and accentuated the hollowness of her thin cheek by pressing it in with one pointed finger.

'To resume,' said Miss Philippa, while her nieces watched her with wondering eyes: 'our dear sister Delia, your poor mamma, repented bitterly for her weakness in marrying a poor man—your papa, children—and being taken away to a dreary place in Central France, where your papa had the management of a very leaden silver-mine, which only produced poverty. The sufferings to which Mr. Julian Riversley exposed your poor mamma were dreadful, my dears. And,' continued Miss Philippa, dotting each eye with her handkerchief, which was not moistened, 'your poor mamma died. She was killed, I might say, by the treatment of your papa; but "De mortuis," Isabella?'

'"Nil nisi bonum,"' sighed the Honourable Isabella.

'Exactly, sister,' continued the Honourable Philippa —'died like several of your unfortunate baby brothers and sisters, my dears; and shortly after—four years exactly, was it not, Isabella ?'

'Three years and eleven months, sister.'

'Thank you, Isabella. Mr. Julian Riversley either fell down that lead-mine or threw himself there in remorse for having deluded a female scion of the ancient house of Dymcoques to follow his fortunes into a far-off land. He was much like you in physique, my dears, but I am glad to say not in disposition—thanks to our training and that of your mamma's spiritual instructor, Mr. Paul Montaigne, to whom dearest Delia entrusted you, and to whom your repentant—I hope—papa gave the sacred charge of bringing you to England to share the calmness of our peaceful home.'

'Peaceful home,' assented Miss Isabella.

'I need hardly tell you, children, that the Riversleys were, or are, nobodies of whom we know nothing— never can know anything.'

'Whatever,' assented Miss Isabella.

'To us they do not exist—neither will they for you, my dears. We believe that Mr. Julian had a sister who married a Mr. Huish ; that is all we know.'

' All we know,' assented Miss Isabella.

' I will say nothing of the tax it has been upon us in connection with our limited income. A grateful country, recognising the services of papa, placed these apartments at our disposal. In consideration of the thoughtfulness of the offer, we accepted these apartments—thirty-five years ago, I think, Isabella ?'

' Thirty-five years and a half, sister.'

' Exactly ; and we have been here ever since, so that we have been spared the unpleasantry of paying a rent. But I need not continue that branch of my subject. What I wish to impress upon you, children, is the fact that in spite of your poor mamma's *mésalliance*, you are of the family of Dymcoques, and that it is your duty to endeavour to raise, and not degrade, our noble house. I think I am following out the proper line of argument, Isabella ?'

' Most accurately, sister.'

' In the event, then, of either of you—at a future time, of course—receiving a proposal of marriage——'

Miss Isabella reopened her fan, and began to use it in a quick, agitated manner.

' It would be your duty to study the interest of

your family, children, and to endeavour to regain
that which your poor mamma lost. To a lady,
marriage——'

Miss Isabella's fan raised quite a draught in the
chilly room, and the white tissue-paper chimney-
apron rustled in the breeze.

'Marriage is the means by which we may recover
the steps lost by those who have gone before; and I
would have you to remember that our position, our
family, our claims to a high descent, warrant our
demanding as a right that we might mate with the
noblest of the land.'

For a moment a curious idea crossed Clotilde's
brain—that her aunts had some thought of entering
the married state; but it passed away on the instant
at the next words.

'Your aunt Isabella and myself might at various
times have entered into alliance with others——'

Miss Isabella's fan went rather slowly now.

'But we knew what was due to our family, and we
said "No!" We sacrificed ourselves in the cause of
duty, and we demand, children, in obedience to our
teaching, that you do the same.'

'Yes, aunt,' said Clotilde demurely.

'An impecunious, poverty-stricken alliance,' continued Miss Philippa, 'is at best a crime, one of which no true woman would be guilty; while an alliance that brings to her family wealth *and* position is one of which she might be proud. You understand, my children?'

'Yes, aunt,' in chorus.

'We—your aunt Isabella and I—of course care little for such things; but we consider that young people of birth and position should, as a matter of duty, look forward to having diamonds, a town house, carriages and servants, pin-money. These are social necessities, children. Plebeians may perhaps consider that they are superfluities, but such democratic notions are the offspring of ignorance. Your grandfather devoted himself to the upholding of Church and State; he was considered worthy of the trust of the Premier of his day; and it is our duty, as his descendants, to hold his name in reverence, and to add to its lustre.'

Marie, as her aunt stopped for breath, wondered in what way her grandfather had benefited his country, and could not help wishing that he had done more to benefit his heirs. Then she half wondered that she had ventured to harbour such a thought, and just then Miss Philippa said blandly :

'I think that will do, Isabella ?'

'Yes, I think that will do,' said that lady, dropping her fan.

'You may retire to the schoolroom, then, my dears,' continued Miss Philippa. 'Clotilde, come here.'

The dark girl, with an unusual flush beneath her creamy skin, crossed the room to her aunt, who laid her hands upon her shoulder, gazed wistfully in her eyes, and then kissed her upon either cheek.

'Wonderfully like your papa, my child,' she said, and she passed her on to Miss Isabella. 'But the Dymcoques' carriage.'

'Ah, yes ! wonderfully like your papa,' sighed Miss Isabella, and she, too, kissed Clotilde upon either cheek. 'But the Dymcoques' carriage.'

'Marie,' said Miss Philippa, 'come here, child.'

Marie rose from her chair, crossed to her aunt, received a hand upon each shoulder and a kiss upon either cheek.

'Yes, your papa's lineaments,' sighed Miss Philippa, passing her on also to Miss Isabella.

'Wonderfully like indeed,' assented Miss Isabella sadly.

'You may retire now, children,' said Miss Philippa. 'You had better resume your practice and studies in the schoolroom. Well, Ruth, why do you not go?'

Poor Ruth had been expecting a similar proceeding towards her, but it did not come about, and she followed her cousins out of the room after each had made a formal curtsey, which was acknowledged by their aunts as if they were sovereigns at a state reception.

'It will cost a great deal, Isabella,' said Miss Philippa, as soon as they were gone.

'Yes, dear; but, as Lady Littletown says, it is an absolute necessity; and it is time they left the school-room for a more enlarged sphere.'

The young ladies went straight to the apartment, where they had passed the greater part of their lives, in company with a green-baize-covered table, a case of unentertaining works of an educational cast, written in that delightfully pompous didactic style considered necessary by our grandfathers for the formation of the youthful mind. There were also selections from Steele and Addison, with Johnson to the extent of 'Rasselas.' Mangnall was there, side by side with Goldsmith, and a goodly array of those speckled-covered school books that used to have such a peculiar smell of size. On a side-table covered with a washed-out red and gray tablecover of that charming draughtboard pattern and cotton fabric, where the gray was red on the opposite side, and in other squares the reds and grays seemed to have married and had neutral offspring, stood a couple of battered and chipped twelve-inch globes, one of which was supposed to be celestial, and the other terrestrial; but time and mildew had joined hand in hand to paint these representations of the spheres with entirely fresh designs, till the terrestrial globe was studded with little dark, damp spots or stars of its own, and fungoid continents had formed themselves on the other amid seas of stain, where nothing but aërial space and constellations should have been.

Ruth entered the schoolroom last, to cross over to where stood on its thin, decrepit legs the harp of other days, in the shape of a most unmusical little piano, which, when opened, looked like some fossil old-world monster of the toad nature, squeezed square and squatting there in a high-shouldered fashion, gaping wide-mouthed, and showing a row of hideous old yellow teeth, the teeth upon which for many a weary hour the girls had practised the ' Battle of Prague,' ' Herz Quadrilles,' and the overture to ' Masaniello,' classical strains that were rather out of tune, and in unwonted guise, consequent upon so many notes being dumb, while what seemed like a row of little imps with round, flat hats performed a kind of excited automatic dance *à la Blondin* upon the wire in the entrails of the fossil toad.

As Ruth crossed and stood leaning with one hand upon the old piano, with her eyelids drooping, and the great tears gathering slowly beneath the heavily-fringed lids, a deep sigh struggled for exit. It was not much to have missed that cold display of something like affection just shown by the ladies to her cousins; but she felt the neglect most sorely, for her tender young heart was hungry for love, and all these many sad years that she had passed in the cheerless

schoolroom, whose one window looked out upon the
dismal fountain in the gloomy court, she had known
so little of what real affection meant.

If she could only have received one word of sympathy just then she would have been relieved, but she
was roused from her sad reverie by a sharp pat upon
the cheek from Clotilde.

'Tears? Why, you're jealous! Here, Rie, the
stupid thing is crying because she was not kissed.'

'Goose!' exclaimed Marie. 'She missed a deal!
Ugh! It's very horrid.'

'Yes,' cried Clotilde. 'Bella's teeth-spring squeaked,
and I thought Pip meant to bite. Here, Ruthy, come
and kiss the places and take off the nasty taste.'

She held out one of her cheeks, and Ruth, whose
face still tingled with the smack she had received,
came forward smiling, threw her arms round her
cousin, and kissed her cheeks again and again.

'Ah, I feel sweeter now!' said Clotilde, pushing
Ruth away. 'Make her do you, Rie.'

Marie laughed unpleasantly as, without being
asked, Ruth, smiling, crossed to her chair and kissed
her affectionately again and again, her bright young

face lighting up with almost childish pleasure, for she was of that nature of womankind whose greatest satisfaction is to give rather than receive.

'There, that will do, baby,' cried Marie, laughing. 'What a gushing girl you are, Ruth!' but she kissed her in return all the same, with the effect that a couple of tears stole from the girl's eyes. 'Mind you don't spoil my lovely dress. Now then, Clo, what does all this mean?'

'Mean?' cried her sister, placing one hand upon the table and vaulting upon it in a sitting position. 'It means—here, Ruth, go down on your knees by the door, and keep your ear by the keyhole. If you let that old hyæna Markes, or either of those wicked old cats, come and hear what we say, I'll buy a sixpenny packet of pins and come and stick them in all over you when you're in bed.'

Ruth ran to the door, knelt down, and placed her ear as she was ordered to do, while her cousin went on:

'It means that the wicked old things are obliged to own at last that we have grown into women, and they want to get us married. Whoop! Lucky for them they do. If they didn't, I'd run away with one of the soldiers. I say, Rie, wasn't that big officer nice?'

'I don't know,' said her sister pettishly. 'I didn't taste him.'

'Who said you did, pig? Diamonds, and carriages, and servants, Rie. I'd have a box at the opera, too, and one at all the theatres. Oh, Rie! wait till I get my chance. I'll keep up the dignity of the family; but when my turn does come, oh! won't I serve those two old creatures out.'

'Dignity of the family, indeed!' cried Marie angrily. 'How dare they speak like they did of poor dear papa, even if he was a Riversley!'

'And the wicked old thing boasting all the time about her Norman descent, and Sir Guyfawkes de Dymcoques. I dare say he was one of the Conqueror's tag-rags, who came to see what he could get.'

'I know poor papa was very handsome.'

'Just like you, Rie,' laughed Clotilde.

'No, he was more like you, Clo,' said her sister quietly. 'I don't see anything to laugh at. Do you suppose I don't know that we are both very beautiful women?'

Clotilde's eyes flashed, and her cheeks began to glow as she saw her sister, in her shabby gingham morning dress, place her hands behind her head, interlacing her fingers and leaning sidewise in an attitude full of natural, unstudied grace.   She looked down at kneeling Ruth.

'We are both handsome girls now, aren't we, Ruth?' she said imperiously.

'Yes, dear, very—very,' said the girl, flushing as she spoke. 'I think you lovely with your beautiful dark eyes, and soft, warm complexions; and you both have such splendid figures and magnificent hair.'

Marie's eyes half closed in a dreamy way, as if some dawning love fancy were there, and an arch smile curled her rich red lip.

She was quite satisfied, and accepted the girl's admiration as her due, hardly moving as Clotilde bounded from the table to the door, listened for a moment, and then, seizing Ruth by the pink, shelly little ear, half dragged her into the room.   Her hot blood showed in her vindictive, fierce way, as she stood threateningly over the kneeling girl.

'Lying little pig,' she hissed, 'how dare you say

such things ! It's your mean-spirited, cringing, favour-currying way. You think we are both as ugly as sin.'

' I don't indeed, indeed I don't !' cried the girl, stung by the charge into indignant remonstrance. ' I think you are both the most beautiful girls I ever saw. Oh, Clotilde! you know what lovely eyes and hair you have.'

' I haven't ; my eyes are dark and my hair is long and coarse.'

' It's beautiful !' cried Ruth, ' isn't it, Marie ? Why, see how everyone turns to look at you both when you are out, in spite of your being so badly dressed.'

' Go back to the door. No, stop,' cried Clotilde, pushing the poor girl's head to and fro as she retained her ear.

' Clotilde dear, you hurt me very much,' sobbed Ruth.

' I'm trying to hurt you,' said Clotilde, showing her white glistening teeth.

' Let her be, Clo.'

' Shan't. Mind your own business.'

' Let her be, I say,' cried Marie, flashing into excitement. ' If you don't loose her I'll scratch you.'

' You daren't,' cried Clotilde, and as her sister's face

turned red her own grew pale. 'Go back to the door and listen, little fibster.'

'I dare,' said Marie, relapsing into her half-dreamy way. 'Come here, Ruthy; I won't have you hurt. It's truth, isn't it? We are beautiful?'

'Yes,' said Ruth, starting to her feet, and joyfully nestling in the arms held out for her, while Marie kissed her with some show of affection. 'Yes, you are both beautiful, and Clotilde knows I would not tell her a story.'

The gratified look had spread by this time to the elder sister's face, and she returned to her position upon the table, where she sat swinging one leg to and fro.

'Go back and listen, Ruthy,' said Marie quietly. 'You are quite right, dear—we are both handsome; and so are you.'

'I?' laughed Ruth, with a merry, innocent look brightening her face; 'oh no!'

'Yes, you are,' said Marie, smoothing her own dark hair. 'You are very nice, and pretty, and sweet, and when I'm married and away from this wicked old poverty-stricken workhouse, you shall come and live with me.'

11—2

'Shall I, Marie?' cried the girl, with the eagerness of a child.

'Yes, dear; and you shall have a handsome husband of your own.'

Ruth laughed merrily.

'What should I do with a husband?'

'Hold your tongue, Rie, and don't stuff the child's head with such nonsense.'

'Child, indeed! why, she is only a year younger than I. Oh! it has been abominable; we have been treated like babies, and I feel sometimes now as if I were only a little girl. But only wait.'

'Yes,' cried Clotilde with a curious laugh, 'only wait.'

'Someone coming,' whispered Ruth, leaping up from the floor where she had been listening, and the child-like obedience to the stern authority in which they had been trained resumed its sway.

Clotilde bounded to the piano, and began to practise a singing lesson, her rich contralto voice rising and falling as she ran up an arpeggio, trying to make it accord with five notes struck together out of tune; Marie darted to a chair, and snatched up a quill pen, inked her forefinger, and bent over a partly written

exercise on composition—a letter addressed to a lady
of title, to be written in the style of Steele ; and Ruth
snatched up a piece of needlework, and began to
sew.   Then the door opened, and Markes, the nurse,
appeared.

'Miss Clotilde and Miss Marie to come to the dining-
room directly.'

' What for, Markes ?' cried Clotilde, pausing in the
middle of a rich-toned run full of delicious melody.

' Come and see.   There, I'll tell you—may as well,
I suppose.   Dressmaker to measure you for some new
frocks.'

' La—ra—ra—ra—ra—ra—ra—rah !' sang Clotilde
in a powerful crescendo, as she swung round upon the
music-stool and then leaped up, while Marie rose
slowly, with a quiet, natural grace.

' Am—am I to come, too ?' said Ruth.

' You ? No. It's them,' said Markes grimly. ' Fine
goings on, 'pon my word.'

' What are fine goings on, Markes ?' cried
Clotilde.

' Why, ordering new dresses. Better buy a new
carpet for one of the bedrooms, and spend a little more

money on the living. I'm getting sick of the pinching and griping ways.'

'I say, Markes, what's for dinner to-day?' exclaimed Marie, on finding the woman in a more communicative mood than usual.

'Cold boiled mutton.'

'Ugh!' ejaculated Clotilde. 'I hate cold mutton. Is there no pudding?'

'Yes; it's pudding day.'

'That's better. What pudding is it?'

Markes shook her head.

'Tell me, and I'll give you a kiss,' said Clotilde.

'If your aunts was to hear you talk like that they'd have fits,' grumbled the woman. 'It's rice-pudding.'

'Baked?'

'No.'

'Boiled in milk?'

'No—plain boiled.'

'Sauce or jam with it?'

'Sauce or jam!' said the woman, in tones of disgust. 'Neither on 'em, but sugar and a bit o' butter; and think yourselves lucky to get that. New dresses, indeed ! It's shameful ; and us in the kitchen half starved !'

'Well, we can't help it,' said Marie. 'I'm sure we don't live any too well.'

'No, you don't,' said the woman, grinning. 'But it does seem a shame to go spending money as they seem to mean to do on you two. I 'spose you're going to be married, ain't you ?'

'I don't know,' said Clotilde. 'Are we ?'

'There, don't ask me. I don't know nothing at all about it, and I shan't speak a word. I only know what I heard them say.'

'Do tell us, Marky dear, there's a dear, good old nursey, and we'll do just as you tell us,' said Clotilde, in a wheedling way.

'You both make haste down, or you'll both have double lessons to get off, so I tell you.'

'But tell us,' said Marie, 'and we'll both give you a kiss.'

'You keep your kisses for your rich husbands, my dears, and I hope you'll like giving 'em—that's all I can say. I told you so : there goes the bell.'

CHAPTER VII.

ECCENTRIC GUESTS.

'THAT'S right—I adore punctuality,' said Dr. Stonor, as John Huish was ushered into the drawing-room of Laurel Hall. For, having mastered the repugnance which had made him feel disposed to send a message to put off his visit, he had chartered a hansom, and run up to the doctor's house.

There was nothing new about it externally, for it was one of those old red-brick buildings that our ancestors knew so well how to contrive, and which they always surrounded with iron railings with great gates about double their height. This was evidently for protection; but why the gates were made so high and the railings so low has never been yet found out.

So John Huish rang and was admitted, starting

slightly on finding himself face to face with Daniel;
but as that individual acted as if they had never met
before, and asked him his name, the visitor felt more
composed, and entered, and was announced.

'My sister, Miss Stonor,' said the doctor. 'Selina,
my dear, this is one of my oldest patients. I pre-
scribed for him for infantile colic when he was a
month old, and lanced his gums at six.'

John Huish found himself face to face with a thin,
prim little lady in tightly-fitting black silk with white
collar and cuffs. She was rather pale, had perfectly
gray hair in smooth bands, and looked mild and wistful,
but she saluted their guest with a quiet smile, and then
he was led off to be introduced to the others present.

'This is Captain Lawdor, Mr. Rawlinson, Mr.
Roberts,' continued the doctor. 'My old friend John
Huish.' And he introduced Huish in turn to a rather
bluff-looking, florid man with gray whiskers; a heavy,
stern and stubborn looking man with iron-gray hair
and a closely-trimmed beard; and a slight, delicate
man with rather a sad expression, which, however, lit
up with a genial smile.

John Huish was very soon engaged with Captain

Lawdor on the question of yachting, and found his new acquaintance somewhat of an enthusiast upon the build and rig of sea-going boats, his preference being for the yawl. But, all the same, he found time to exchange a few words with the thin, pensive-looking Mr. Roberts, who chatted about the politics of the hour, and with Mr. Rawlinson, whose speech quite carried out the stubborn appearance of his knotty forehead and short iron-gray hair. He was very indignant about a railway accident mentioned in the daily paper, and gave it as his opinion that there would be no safety until heavy penalties were inflicted upon the companies, or else until the lines were in the hands of the Government.

Then Daniel came in and announced dinner, and Mr. Roberts taking down Miss Stonor, Huish found himself with the doctor.

'Patients not well enough to show up, doctor?' he said quietly, as they went towards the dining-room.

'Eh?'

'I said, "Patients not well enough to show up?"'

'Hist! Don't mention them,' said the doctor;

and Huish gave a sigh of relief as he thought how
much better the dinner would pass off without such
company.

A minute later and they were seated at table, John
Huish on the doctor's right, and the captain on his
right again. The stubborn, heavy man was upon
Miss Stonor's right, and the pensive-looking man
facing Huish. Grace was said, the cover of the soup-
tureen was lifted with a flourish by Daniel, and Miss
Stonor ladled out the clear brown *julienne*, half hidden
herself behind the tureen, till all were helped but
Mr. Rawlinson and the doctor.

Mr. Rawlinson passed his hands through his iron-
gray hair, and smiled as he watched the ladle go
down into the steaming fluid and come up again to
be emptied into the plate held by Daniel.

'And so, Rawlinson, you would heavily fine the
companies?' said the doctor.

'Indeed I would,' was the reply. 'Would you
mind, Miss Stonor,' he continued insinuatingly, 'half
a ladleful more? Delicious soup. Thanks.'

Miss Stonor smiled, and the soup was placed before
him, when, to the amazement of Huish, Mr. Rawlin-

son sent his chair back with a quick motion, deftly
lifted the soup-plate on to the Turkey carpet, and, as
if it were a footpan, composedly placed the toes of
his patent-leather shoes therein.

Miss Stonor did not move a muscle—she might
have been a disciple of Daniel; while the doctor said
quietly: 'Head hot, Rawlinson?'

'Yes, very,' was the reply, as the eccentric guest
smiled and nodded.

'I'd go and lie down for an hour,' said the doctor
gently.

'Would you—would you?' said Mr. Rawlinson,
smiling pleasantly. 'Well, I will.'

'Come and join us presently if you feel better,' said
the doctor.

'Certainly I will,' said Mr. Rawlinson. 'Miss
Stonor, you'll excuse me?'

Miss Stonor bowed, and he turned upon Daniel.

'A napkin, Daniel,' he said rather severely. 'I
cannot leave the room with my shoes in this state.'

He lifted his feet from the soup-plate as he spoke,
and sat with his legs at right angles to his body,
while in the most matter-of-fact way Daniel stooped

down, wiped the patent-leather shoes, and, sticking his thumbs into his armholes, Mr. Rawlinson calmly left the room.

'Suppose you ease off a little to the left, Roberts,' said the doctor, as the soup-plate was removed. 'Rawlinson will not be back to dinner.'

'No,' said the captain, smiling. 'Poor fellow!' he continued, turning to Huish; 'you would not have thought he was a little wrong, I suppose?'

'Indeed I should not,' said Huish eagerly.

'No,' said the captain. 'He looks as sane as I am; but he breaks out now and then, poor fellow!'

Just then Daniel was helping the guests to sherry, and Huish noticed that the captain's glass was passed.

It seemed strange, but the conversation took off his attention, and he thought no more of it till Daniel set down the decanter, when, picking up the little round roll that lay by his napkin, the captain threw it with so good an aim that he hit the solid servitor a smart crack on the back of the head.

'Now, Captain Lawdor,' said Miss Stonor, in tones of bland reproof, 'have I not told you that if you will persist in doing that you must not dine with us?'

'Hush! hush!' he whispered apologetically. 'Don't scold me before the company. Poor fellow! I don't like to see a new patient upset. That fellow always passes me with the sherry.'

John Huish's countenance was so ludicrous at being taken for a new patient that the doctor exchanged glances with his sister, and it was all they could do to keep from bursting into a hearty fit of laughter. The doctor, however, suppressed his, and said quietly :

'My sister is quite right, Lawdor, and you must get rid of that habit.'

The captain drew out his pocket-handkerchief, shed tears, wiped his eyes, and ended by taking out a half-crown, which he slipped into Daniel's hand as he removed his empty plate.

John Huish felt a little disturbed as he saw the real state of affairs, but he tried to appear at his ease, and plunged into conversation with Miss Stonor, not, however, before he had directed an uneasy glance or two at his quiet, pensive companion across the table, who, however, was carrying on a discussion with the doctor.

Huish could not help thinking of the knives as the captain turned to him with a pleasant smile lighting up his ruddy face, from which all trace of sorrow had now passed.

' That's a nasty trick,' he said ; ' but I never knew a man without some bad habit or another. I could hit him, though, with a biscuit at fifty paces.'

' Indeed,' said Huish.

' Yes, that I could. If I've hit Daniel once, I've done it a hundred times. But we were talking about yachting. Now, I've got a plan for a ship which I have submitted to the Admiralty.'

' Oh,' said Huish to himself, ' here, then, is the sore place.' Then aloud, ' Indeed !'

' Yes ; a splendid idea. But, by the way, you know how fond we sailors are of talking about pitching a biscuit ?'

' To be sure,' said Huish.

' Excuse me a few moments. A sailor always eats when he has a chance. May be called on deck at any moment. Would you oblige me ?' said the captain suddenly to Huish.

' I beg your pardon, certainly,' said Huish ; and,

partly from habit, he placed his glass in his eye and brought it to bear on the speaker.

'This is rather a good story—eh, doctor ?'

'Yes. Go on, Captain Lawdor.'

'Well, you see, I had been communicating with the Admiralty for six years about my invention when — would you oblige me by taking that glass out of your eye?' said the captain, breaking off short in his narrative. 'It irritates me, and makes me feel as if I must throw something at it.'

John Huish's eyeglass dropped inside his vest, while, in spite of all his efforts to master his emotions, he glanced uneasily at the door.

'But you would not do anything so rude, Lawdor,' said the doctor gravely, as he fixed his eye upon the captain.

'Thank you, doctor. No ; of course I would not. I should be extremely sorry to insult a patient of yours.'

Huish began to feel for his glass, but remembered himself, and listened eagerly to the captain, while Mr. Roberts seemed to have sunk into a pensive, thoughtful state, paying no heed to what was going on at the table.

'If I had danced attendance in Whitehall once,' said Captain Lawdor, 'I had hung about that entrance a thousand times, and it was fill up forms, make minutes, present petitions to my Lords, address this department and come back to that, till it nearly drove me—till,' he added hastily, 'I was very wroth with them, and one day—let me see, I think I told you,' he continued, rolling up a piece of new bread into a marble, 'that I was an excellent shot with a biscuit?' and he stared hard at Huish.

'Yes, you did,' said Huish, smiling.

'Don't laugh, sir,' exclaimed the captain. 'This is not a ribald jest.'

'Breakers ahead, captain,' said the doctor, holding his glass to be refilled.

'To be sure, of course, doctor. Wear ship—you are listening, sir?'

'With the greatest attention,' replied Huish, who was becoming reconciled to his position.

'Well, sir, one day I went with my pockets filled with the roundest, smallest, and hardest ships' biscuits I could procure, and—you are not attending, Roberts,' he exclaimed, filliping the bread marble at John Huish's *vis-à-vis*, who bowed and smiled.

'Well, sir, as I told you, I went loaded with the biscuits, and marched straight into a board room, or a committee room, or something of the kind, and there I stormed them for quite ten minutes before they got me out. Ha, ha, ha! I emptied my pockets first, and the way I rattled the biscuits on one bald-headed fellow's pate was something to remember. I did not miss him once, Mr. Huish,' he said, turning sharply round.

'Indeed?' he said, smiling.

'In—deed, in—deed,' said the captain. 'It was such a head! He was one of those youngish men whose heads are so aggravatingly white and smooth and shiny that they do not look bald, but perfectly naked. He was a Junior Lord of the Admiralty, and I declare to you, sir, that his head was perfectly indecent till I coloured it a little with the biscuits.'

'Yes, an amusing story,' said the doctor, as the dinner went on. 'Come, Roberts, you are very quiet. Have a glass of that dry champagne?'

'And once again I see that brow,' said Mr. Roberts in a low, soft, sweet voice : 'no bridal wreath is there, a widow's sombre cap conceals—thank you, doctor,' he continued, sighing as he altered the position of the glass.

The dinner passed off without any further incident, save that Mr. Rawlinson returned looking very quiet and calm, and in time for the second course, of which he partook heartily, rising after the dessert to open the door for Miss Stonor to leave the room, and all in the most natural manner.

'Suppose we go into my room a bit now,' said the doctor. 'We can have a cigar there;' and Daniel entering at that moment with coffee, it was taken into the doctor's sanctum, the patients following the tray, the doctor hanging back with his principal guest.

'Well, my dear John, do you think you are going mad now?'

'No,' was the quick reply.

'Of course not. You see now what even a mild form of mania is.'

'I do,' was the reply. 'But look here, doctor,' said

Huish earnestly; 'this feeling has troubled me terribly just lately.'

'And why?' said the doctor sharply, for Huish hesitated.

'Well, the fact is, doctor, it is possible that I may marry some day, and I felt——'

'Yes, of course, I know,' said the doctor; 'you felt, and quite rightly, that it would be a crime to marry some sweet young girl if you had the seeds of insanity waiting to develop themselves in your brain.'

'Yes, doctor, that was it.'

'My dear John Huish, you are a bit of a favourite of mine, and I like you much.'

'Thank you, doctor, I——'

'I made the acquaintance of your father and mother in a peculiar manner, and they have always trusted me since.'

'Yes; I have heard something of it from it my father, but——'

'Just hold your tongue and listen to me, sir. You have, I am sure, chosen some sweet, gentle, good girl; nothing else would suit you. So all I have to say is this : your brain is as right as that of any man living.

Marry her, and the sooner the better. I like these young marriages, and hang all those musty old fogies who preach about improvidence and so many hundreds a year! Marry early, while you and the woman you love are in the first flush of your youth and vigour. It's nature—it's holy—and the good God smiles upon it. Damn it all, sir! it makes me savage to see a wretched, battered old fellow being chosen by a scheming mother of the present day as a husband for her child. Money and title will not compensate for youth. It's a wrong system, John Huish, a wrong system. I'm a doctor, and I ought to know. Marry, then, my dear boy, as soon as you like, and God bless you!'

'Thank you, doctor, thank you,' said Huish, smiling. ' But I say, doctor, if it is not impertinence, why didn't you marry young?'

'Because I was a fool. I wanted to make money and a name in my profession, and did not calculate what would be the cost. They cost me thirty years, John Huish, and now I am an old fogey, content to try and do some good among my poor patients. But come away; they will think me rude. Eh, going now? Well, I will not say stop, as you have so far to go back. One more word : think your head's screwed on right now?'

'Yes, doctor.'

'So do I. If it ever goes wrong, come to me, and I'll turn it back.'

But John Huish did not feel quite satisfied, all the same.

CHAPTER VIII.

IN BORROWED PLUMES.

THERE was a good deal of excitement in the Hampton
Court dovecote, and a general touching up of plumage,
for Lady Littletown, who resided at Hampton, so as
to be near her dear old friend Lady Anna Maria
Morton, who had rooms up a narrow dingy stone
staircase in the corner of a cloistered court, in the
private apartments at the Palace, had sent out cards
for her dinner-party and 'at home.'

Lady Littletown was rich, and her position in the
society of the neighbourhood was that of queen. A
widow for many years, she was always thinking of
marriage. Not for herself. She had been through
the fire, and found it hot. In fact, she bore her
mental scars to her elderly age, for it was a well-

known fact that the late Viscount Littletown was the extreme opposite of an angel. He had possessed a temper which grew and blossomed in wild luxuriance, and the probabilities are that he inoculated her ladyship with this peculiarity of spirit, for more than one of her domestics had been known to have declared that they would not live with the 'old devil' any longer.

This was very wicked, and the domestic young ladies who had made use of such expressions were much to be censured. But certain it was that the Viscountess was far from perfect, and that she was an inveterate match-maker.

Probably she was of opinion that it would be a pleasant little piece of revenge on human nature to inveigle as many of her sex as possible on to the stormy sea of matrimony. At all events, a good many fashionable marriages resulted from plans laid by her ladyship and her female friends.

Lady Littletown's friends were many, and included Lady Millet, whom she always addressed as 'my dear,' in spite of a pique which had arisen consequent upon the latter marrying her eldest daughter to that wealthy *parvenu*, Mr. Frank Morrison.

Now, according to Lady Littletown's code, this was not correct. Dear friends as they had been, Lady Millet should have obtained her help, seeing that marriages were her *métier;* but she had obstinately gone her own way, invited her to the wedding, and latterly had actually shown that she was scheming something about two gentlemen whom Lady Littletown had marked down for her own—to wit, Lord Henry Moorpark and Mr. Elbraham, the great financier.

'But, poor thing! she did not know how to manage Elbraham,' said Lady Littletown to herself; 'and as for dear Lord Henry, not if I know it, dearest. I think I can manage that, and you may marry pink-and-white wax-doll Gertrude to someone else.'

So her ladyship issued her cards most discriminatingly and well, in her determination to let no rival in her circle interfere with her rights as high-priestess of Hymen to her dearest friends.

Lady Littletown's invitations on this occasion had included the Honourable Misses Dymcox and their nieces Clotilde and Marie Riversley; and, like Cinderella of the story, Ruth had rather a hard time with her cousins. For, to the astonishment of the latter, a fashionable dressmaker had been down expressly from London, and their excitement over the handsome robes that had arrived knew no bounds.

Their aunts had been a long time in making a move, and divers had been the consultations with Viscountess Littletown and Lady Anna Maria Morton. When at last that step was taken, it was with firmness and judgment combined.

Poor Ruth was divided between longings to go to the dinner-party and admiration of her cousins' appearance, which, when they stood at last dressed, an hour before the time, parading the shabby bedroom and sweeping the skimpy pieces of Kidderminster carpet here and there with their stiff trains, was dazzling.

Certainly a handsomer pair of women rarely graced a party, and the Honourable Misses Dymcox, after a careful inspection through their square florid goldedged eyeglasses, uttered sighs of satisfaction.

For the *modiste* had done her duty well. The dresses were in the latest style, they fitted to perfection, and the girls' youth and the luxuriance of their hair quite made up for the want of jewellery to enhance their charms.

The Honourable Misses Dymcox were almost as excited as their nieces, for they, too, managed to get dressed an hour before time in their lavender silk straight-up-and-down garments, to which were tacked a few old pieces of very yellow lace, supposed to be an heirloom, but certainly very unattractive, whatever it may have been when young.

A very weak cup of tea had been taken, the elder ladies being in fear and trembling all the while.

'No, no, children, wait!' exclaimed Miss Philippa. 'Joseph, put down the cups, and tell Markes to bring here two large pocket-handkerchiefs.'

In due time Markes appeared.

'Now, children,' said Miss Philippa, 'stand up. Markes, have the goodness to tie a handkerchief by two of the corners just under the young ladies' chins. It would be ruin to those dresses if they spilt any of their tea.'

'If you please, aunt, I don't want any tea,' said Clotilde.

'Neither do I, aunt,' said Marie.

'Hush, children! You must take your tea. It is imperative that you should enter Lady Littletown's drawing-room calm, self-possessed, and without any sign of being flushed. Markes, tie on those handkerchiefs.'

A red spot burned in the girls' cheeks as they submitted to the childish indignity, and when they were duly provided with their bibs they were allowed to drink their thin, washy, half-cold tea, exchanging glances the while, for their emancipation had not yet arrived.

'Ruth, ring the bell,' said Miss Philippa, as soon as the tea was finished, and the handkerchiefs, which had been rising and falling in a troubled fashion, had been removed.

'Take away these teacups, Joseph,' said Miss Philippa. 'Has the carriage arrived?'

'No, mum. It wants more than half an hour to the time. Buddy hasn't been in yet.'

'Hush! Silence!' cried Miss Philippa harshly; 'and dear me, Joseph, there is a large place on the back of your head not powdered.'

Joseph was heard to mutter something, and then

he went forth in his best livery of pale blue with
yellow facings and black knee-breeches, to finish his
toilet for the night.

'Oh, here you are, then,' exclaimed Joseph, upon
reaching his pantry, a peculiarly close, stuffy little
room, smelling very strongly of sink, and furnished
with two cupboards, a bracket flap, and what looked
like a third detached cupboard, but which was really
the turn-up bedstead on which Joseph slept.

'Yes, here I am, Joey,' said a husky-voiced little
red-nosed man, with a very blotchy, pimply face, to
wit Isaac Buddy, the sole proprietor of a roomy old-
fashioned Clarence fly, which was drawn by a very
small shambling horse.

This conveyance was Mr. Isaac Buddy's means of
livelihood, for it was to let, as his cards said, 'by the
day, night, or job,' and the hiring of Mr. Isaac Buddy's
fly meant not only, as a matter of course, the hire of
the horse to draw it, but of Mr. Isaac Buddy himself.

For, out of deference to the feelings and aristocratic ideas of certain of the ladies residing in the
private apartments, Mr. Buddy had become an actor,
who played many parts, and though the fiction was

perfectly well understood, nobody ever thought of
smiling if they saw Mr. Isaac Buddy in a hat with a
tarnished gold band on Mondays as Lady Anna
Maria Morton's coachman, or in a hat with a silver
band on Tuesday, as Miss Tees', or on Wednesday in
a very hard shiny glazed hat without any nap, as
Mrs. Mongloff's, or on other days in costumes to
suit.

The Clarence fly of course remained the same, but
it was always disguised in a more sounding name,
and became ' the carriage.'

'There ain't a drop o' nothing about handy, is
there, Joey?' said Mr. Buddy, as the thin footman
set the tray down upon the bracket-flap.

'No, that there ain't,' said Joseph, 'without you'd
like the pot filled up and have a cup o' tea.'

'G'orn with yer.   Did you ever know me wash
myself out with warm water?   How's the old gals?'

'Old style,' replied Joseph; 'but I say, Buddy, just
cast your eye round as they're getting in : the young
ladies have been done up to rights.'

'I wish someone would find the money to get my
old fly done up to rights,' said Mr. Buddy, who,

apparently quite at home, was standing before a
shaving-glass hung against the wall, persuading, with
Joseph's brush, a couple of very obstinate little
whiskers to stand out straight forward in the direction
their owner wished. ''Spose there'll be a wedding,
then, some day.'

' Well, I dunno,' said Joseph.

' Looks like it, if they're having 'em fresh painted,'
said Mr. Buddy, who now touched up his very greasy
gray hair, making it stick up in points, in unconscious
imitation of that of a clown.

' Here, you'd better look sharp, old man,' said
Joseph, ' they're all ready and waiting, and time's
getting on.'

' Which we ain't, Joey, or we should be doing
better than we are, eh ?'

' Ah, we should,' said Joseph, making a powder-box
squeak as he unscrewed the top ; and then taking out
the puff, he placed a tea-cloth over his shoulders, and
gave his hair a few dabs. ' Now then, old man.
Have the tea-cloth on ?'

' Ah, you may as well,' was the reply ; and the cloth
having been adjusted by Joseph, the little man stood

blinking solemnly while his dingy hair was duly powdered and turned white.

'Why, you might stand a bit o' wilet powder cump'ny nights, Joey,' said the flyman, solemnly removing a little white meal from amongst the ruddy pimples of his face with the corner of the cloth in regular use for wiping the tea and breakfast service.

'How am I to stand best vi'let powder out o' what they allow?' replied Joseph. 'Flour's just as good, and don't cost me nothing. Now then, look sharp.'

As he spoke Joseph pulled open a drawer, from which he drew a drab great-coat, inside which the little man placed himself, for it was manifestly so much too large that he could hardly be said to have put it on. Then a blue hat-box was pushed off the top of one of the cupboards, out of which a rather ancient hat was extricated, and mounted by the fly-man, whose head seemed to have become suddenly wonderfully small; for it was an imposing structure of beaver with very curly brims, apparently kept from coming uncurled by a rigging or series of stays of tarnished silver cord, which ran from the lining up to a Panjandrum-like round button at the top, also of

tarnished silver; while a formidable-looking and very
spiky black cockade rose something like a patent
ventilator from one side.

'That's about the ticket, ain't it, Joey?' said the
little man, shaking his head so as to get the big hat
in a good state of balance, and buttoning himself to
the chin.

' Yes, that will do, old man.'

' The ladies want to know if the carriage has come,
Joseph,' said Markes, suddenly making her appearance.

'Which you may take your solemn oath it ain't,'
said Mr. Buddy, 'for not one inch will that there
horse stir till I wakes him up.'

' Then do for goodness' sake, man, look sharp and
fetch it,' exclaimed Markes. ' I'm sure it's past the
time !'

' Wants five minutes,' said Mr. Buddy, nodding his
head, and having to dart one hand up to save the hat,
which came down over his nose, and would have continued its course to the floor. ' I say, your old coachman must have had a head like a bull, to have worn
that hat without stuffing. There, I'm off. Soon be

back. I say, though,' he whispered, thrusting back his head, and this time holding on by the rigging of the hat, 'if it comes to a wedding, the old gals ought to stand some new togs.'

Within a quarter of an hour Mr. Isaac Buddy, who had entered the private apartments as flyman, and came out the Honourable Misses Dymcox's coachman, was at the door with the transformed fly. The ladies were duly packed inside, with many tremors as to their dresses, and Joseph, also in a drab greatcoat and a fearful and wonderful hat—the twin-brother of that upon Mr. Buddy's head—mounted to the seat. Then the carriage jingled and jangled off— a dashing brougham and pair, with flashing lights and the windows down, rattling by them, making Buddy's nervous nag shy to the near side, as if he meant to mount the side walk out of the way.

' Rie,' whispered Clotilde, with her ruddy lips touching her sister's ear.

' Yes.'

' That funny little officer was inside.'

' Yes,' muttered Marie to herself, ' and the tall one as well ; and you know it. I wonder who they are ?'

CHAPTER IX.

THE SLAVE OF FORTUNE.

'I say, look here! You know, Litton, I'm the last
man on earth to complain ; but you know, d—n it,
you don't do your duty by me.'

'You don't give me credit for what I do do,
Elbraham, 'pon my soul you don't !' said the gentleman addressed—a rather fashionably-dressed, stylish
young fellow of eight-and-twenty or thirty, whose
hair was closely cropped in the latest style, his well-
worn clothes scrupulously brushed, and his hands
particularly white.

As he answered he screwed his glass very tightly
into his eyes and gazed at the first speaker—a little,
pudgy, high-shouldered man, with a very short neck
and a very round head, slightly bald. He was care-

13—2

fully dressed, and a marked point in his attire was the utter absence of everything in the shape of jewellery or ornament. His fat white hands did not display so much as a ring; and though a slight prominence in his vest proclaimed the presence of a watch, it was attached to his person by a guard of the finest black silk. His countenance, however, did not match with the refinement of his attire, for it betrayed high living and sensual indulgence. There was an unpleasant look, too, about his eyes; and if to the least cultured person he had asserted in the most emphatic manner that he was a gentleman, it would not have been believed.

But, all the same, he was a man of mark, for this was Samuel Elbraham, the financier, the man who was reputed to have made hundreds of thousands by his connection with the Khedive. Men in society and on 'Change joked about Elbraham, and said that he was a child of Israel, who went down into Egypt and spoiled the Egyptians for everybody's buying but his own. They called him Potiphar, too, and made it a subject of jest that there was no Potiphar's wife; but they also said that it did not matter, for

these were days when people had arisen who knew
not Joseph.

Then they laughed, and wondered whether Potiphar
of old went in for a theatre, and supplied rare subsidies
of hard cash to a manager, and was very fond of
taking parties of friends to his private-box to witness
the last new extravaganza, after the said friends had
dined with him and drunk his champagne.

Somehow or other, it was the friends who ate his
dinners and drank his champagne that made the
most jokes about him ; but though these witticisms,
real or would be, came round to him at times, they
troubled him very little.

The conversation above commenced took place in
Mr. Elbraham's library, at the riverside residence at
Twickenham, the handsomely-furnished place that he,
the celebrated converted Israelite, had taken of Lord
Washingtower, when a long course of ill-luck on the
turf had ended in nearly placing his lordship under
the turf, for rumour said that his terrible illness was
the result of an attempt to rid himself of his woes by
a strong dose of a patent sedative medicine.

As Mr. Elbraham spoke he hitched up his shoulders,

thrust his hands into his pockets, and walked up and down in front of the books he never read.

'Not give you credit for what you do?' he retorted. 'Why, what do you mean?'

'Don't talk to me like that, Elbraham, please. I'm not your servant.'

'Hang it all, then, what the devil are you? I pay you regular wages.'

'No. Stop, please. I accept a regulated stipend from you, Elbraham.'

'Oh, very good! let's have it like that, then, Mr. Rarthur Litton. I took you up, same as I did your bills, when you were so hard hit that you didn't know where to go for a fiver. You made certain proposals and promises to me, and, I ask you, what have you done?'

'More than you give me credit for,' was the reply, rather sullenly made.

'You dine with me, you sleep here, and make this place your home whenever you like; and when I look for your help, as I expected, I find that your name is in the papers as the secretary to some con-founded Small Fish Protection Society, or as managing director of the Anti-Soap and Soda Laundry Company.'

'I'm sure I've done my duty by you, Mr. Elbraham,' said the young man hotly. 'If you want to quarrel and get rid of me, say so.'

'I don't want to quarrel, and I don't mean to quarrel, Mr. Rarthur Litton. I made a bargain with you, and I mean to keep you to it. You boasted to me of your high connections and your *entrée* into good society, and undertook to introduce me into some of the best families, so that I might take the position that my wealth enables me to hold. Now, then, please, have I paid up like a man?'

'Yes ; you have,' was the sulky response.

'And you've taken jolly good care to draw more than was your due. Now, what have you done?'

'Well, I taught you to dress like something different to a cad.'

'Humph! You did knock off my studs and rings and things.'

'And I've dined with you till I've got you to be fit to eat your meals in a Christianlike manner.'

'Look here, Mr. Rarthur, sir,' said Elbraham hotly, 'is that meant as a sneer?'

'No; of course not.'

'Oh!'

'Then I wanted time to get these things in proper course. Well, come now, I did get you the invitation to Lady Littletown's.'

'Yes; to a beggarly dinner with an old woman at Hampton. Are you going to dine there?'

'I? No! I come in afterwards at the "at home."'

'Ah! I wanted to talk to you about that affair to-night. You promised without my consent.'

'Of course I did. It was a great chance.'

'A great chance?'

'Of course. You don't know how big a thing it is to be.'

'Bah! stuff! rubbish! A feed given to all the old pensioned tabbies at Hampton Court.'

'Don't you make any mistake, sir. There'll be some big people there.'

'Big! Why, I could buy up dozens of them.'

'Their incomes, perhaps, Mr. Elbraham, but not

their position and their *entrée* to good society. Sir, you could not even buy mine.'

' But I could your bills,' said the other, with a grin.

' And hold them over me, you wretched little cad !' said the young man to himself. Then aloud :

' I can assure you, Mr. Elbraham, that this dinner will give you the step you wanted. Lady Littletown stands very high in society. The Duchess of Redesby will be there, and Lord Henry Moorpark.'

' What ! old Apricot—old yellow and ripe ?' said Elbraham with a chuckle.

' Lord Henry Moorpark is a thorough specimen of an English nobleman, Mr. Elbraham,' said the secretary stiffly ; ' and I consider that if the only thing I had done was to gain you an introduction to him, I should have earned all the wages, as you call them, that you have condescended to pay me.'

' Yes, of course—yes, to be sure. There, there, don't be so hot and peppery, Litton. I'm a bit put out this morning. By the way, would you have the brougham and pair or one horse ?'

' Pair, decidedly,' said the young man.

' You'll not go with me ?'

'No; I come afterwards. You shall bring me back if you will.'

'Yes; of course. I'll put some cigars in the pocket. Would you wear the diamond studs?'

'*No.* Not a ring, even. Go in black, and hardly speak a word. Do nothing but look the millionaire. The simpler you dress, my dear sir, the richer they will think you.'

'My dear Litton, you're a treasure—damme, that you are, sir! I say, look here: you don't happen to want five, or ten, or twenty this morning, do you?'

Mr. Arthur Litton did happen to want twenty, not five or ten; and a couple of crisp notes were thrust into his hand.

'Well, I suppose it's all right, Litton. I shall look out for you there, then; but it's a deuce of a way to go.'

'It's worth going to, if it were double the distance, I can assure you. You have money; you want position.'

'All right, then; that's settled. I'm going to the City now. Are you going in?'

'No, thanks; I shall sit down and do a little writing.'

'Very good ; you'll find the cigars on the shelf.'

'What, those cigars?' He spoke with a slight emphasis on the 'those.' 'No, thanks; they have too strong a flavour of a hundred-pound bill.'

'What do you mean?'

'Forty pounds in cash, forty in old pale East India sherry, and twenty in weeds.'

'You're an artful one, you are, Litton—'pon my soul you are. Deuced artful,' said Mr. Elbraham, with a curious puckering about the corners of his eyes, intended to do duty for a smile. 'But that reminds me, Huish's bill falls due to-morrow— hundred pounds ; mustn't forget that. Here, pull out your case.'

He unlocked a little cabinet with a tiny key, and opened two or three drawers full of cigars, each with a paper band round its middle.

'Which is it to be?'

The young man smiled, and filled his case, selecting one as well for present smoking. The cabinet was reclosed ; there was an interchange of nods ; Elbra-

ham went off to the station; Litton sat down and
wrote a letter, after which he made a little study of
a time-table, hurried off, and, catching a train, was
soon after [on his way to Hampton, where he was
just in time to catch Lady Littletown entering her
carriage for a drive.

'Ah, *mon cher* Arthur!' she exclaimed; 'you nearly
missed me.   There, come in, and I'll take you part of
your way back.'

Litton mounted beside her ladyship, and took his
seat as invited.

'Drive slowly,' cried her ladyship; and as the
handsome barouche, with its well-appointed pair of
bays, went gaily along the pleasant river-side road
towards the Palace, Lady Littletown turned her sharp
dark eyes searchingly upon her companion.

She was one of those elderly ladies upon whom
the effect of time seems to be that of making them
sharper and possessed of a keener interest in worldly
matters, and one in whose aquiline features there was
ample promise of her proving to be a most implacable
enemy if offended.   Too cautious to allow her heart
to be stirred by instincts of an amatory nature, she

had found consolation in looking after the matrimonial business of others ; and hence her interest in her companion of the hour.

' Well ?' she said sharply ; ' what news ?'

' I've fixed him for certain. He would have backed out, but for a bit of a chat this morning.'

' Then the nasty, scaly, slippery gold-fish will really come ?'

' Yes.'

' Not disappoint me as he did Judy Millet ?'

' You may depend upon him this time.'

' Good boy, good boy. Now, look here, Arthur : you are behaving very well over this, and if the affair comes off as I wish, and you behave very nicely, I'll see next what I can do by way of finding you a wife with a snug fortune ; only you must not be too particular about her looks.'

' I leave myself in your ladyship's hands.'

' There, now you may get down. I'm going to make two or three calls in the Palace.'

' One moment, Lady Littletown,' said Litton eagerly ; ' I'm just starting a society for the preservation of ancient trees and old——'

'Now, *mon cher*, that will do,' said the old lady
decidedly. 'You know I never give money or——'

'I only ask for your name as a patroness or sup-
porter.'

'And you will not have it; so now be a good boy,
and go. I've got your name down upon my tablets,
Arthur, so wait your time. Stop!'

The horses were checked; the footman descended
and opened the door, rattling the steps loudly;
Arthur Litton leaped out, raised his hat; Lady
Littletown kissed the tips of her gloved fingers to
him, and the carriage passed on.

'I wonder whether she will,' said the young man,
as he walked towards the station. 'However, we
shall see.'

CHAPTER X.

'My income, my dears, just suffices for my wants,' said Lady Littletown; 'and I have never anything to spare for charities and that sort of thing.'

So said her ladyship to her aristocratic friends living in pinched circumstances in the private apartments; and it may or may not have been intended for a hint not to try and borrow money.

'One would like to be charitable and to give largely, but what with one's household expenses and the horses and carriages, and my month in town in the height of the season, I really sometimes find myself obliged to ask his late lordship's agent for a few hundreds in advance of the time when the rents are due. But then, you see, one owes so much to one's position.'

The Honourable Misses Dymcox said one certainly did ; Lady Anna Maria Morton, who had been longing for a new silk evening dress for three years, said the same ; and, thoroughly feeling it to be a fact, Lady Littletown tried to pay honourably what she owed to society by rigidly living up to the last penny of her fairly handsome income in the pleasant mansion near Hampton Court.

She gave about four dinner-parties in the course of the year, and afterwards received.

This was one of her special parties for a special purpose, and when the last of her fifteen guests had arrived and been looked at through her great gold eyeglass held with the left hand, while the tips of the fingers of the right were given in assurance of her being 'so delighted,' her ladyship proceeded to marshal her forces for the procession to the dining-room.

'Here's what it is to be a lone widow !' she exclaimed playfully. 'Moorpark, might I ask you to take the foot of the table ?—Miss Marie Riversley.'

Lord Henry had murmured to himself a good deal about being dragged down all the way from

St. James's Square to Hampton just at a time when
his heart told him that he ought to be married, and
though terribly dissatisfied with the success which had
attended his attentions to Gertrude Millet, his brain
was full of her bright, refined features. He, however,
now advanced, quite the handsome, stately gentleman, with a pleasant, benevolent look upon his thin
face, and at once entered into conversation with the
dark beauty to whom he had been introduced.

'Mr. Elbraham,' continued Lady Littletown, in a
confidential whisper, as she inspected him as if he
were for sale, 'would you oblige me ?—Miss Dymcox's
niece.'

The reputed millionaire started, and a scowl began
to dawn in his face, for the name Dymcox brought
up the faces of the honourable sisters ; but as he was
led to dark, glowing, southern-faced Clotilde, the
scowl reached no farther than its dawn, and the
ruddy sun of his coarse round face rose out of the fog,
and beamed its satisfaction upon the handsome girl.

'Oh, I say, Glen, what a shame!' whispered little
Dick Millet to his chosen companion, who, consequent upon his being an officer and the friend of dear

Lady Millet's son, had been invited, like his major, to the feast.

Dick began grinding his white teeth in the corner, where he had been making eyes at Clotilde and Marie in turn, whichever looked in his direction; and for the moment he seemed as if he were going to tear either his curly hair or the dainty exotic from his button-hole.

'Hush! be quiet,' was the reply.

'Hurrah! viva!' whispered Dick again. 'The Black Douglas is being tacked on to that old scrag.'

'That old scrag' was the Honourable Philippa Dymcox, and 'the Black Douglas' Major Edward Malpas, who, probably from disappointment in connection with a late marriage, was contemplatively watching Clotilde; but his courtesy was perfect as he bent toward the Honourable Philippa.

'Now there's that other old she-dragon, Glen,' whispered Dick. 'Oh, I say, it's too bad of the old woman! I won't, that I won't. I didn't come here to be treated so, and if she says I'm to march in that dreadful skeleton I'll be taken ill and make a bolt of it. I say, Marcus,' he continued, 'my nose is going to bleed ;' and as he spoke he took out his delicately-scented pocket-handkerchief.

'Captain Glen, will you take in the Honourable Isabella Dymcox ?' said Lady Littletown, showing just a trifle of gold setting as she smiled.

Marcus Glen told the truth when he said he would be most happy, for he recognised in the lady of the old-fashioned lavender poplin one of the companions of Clotilde and Marie in their walk in the Palace gardens.

Dick Millet thrust his scented cambric back into the pocket of his silk-lined coat, and after a glance at the ladies, either of whom he longed to take in to dinner, he had a look round the room to see which would be the most eligible dinner-table companion of those that were left ; but to his disgust he began to find that he was being left entirely in the cold, for the hostess, with all the skill of one who has well made her plans beforehand, was rapidly finishing her arrangements.

'It's enough to make any man's nose bleed, and compel him to bolt,' muttered the handsome little fellow, who had got himself up in the most irreproachable manner, having even been to town that afternoon on purpose to place himself in a hair-dresser's hands.

'Hang it all! am I nobody?'

It was hard work getting hold of the ends, but Dick managed to give a vicious twist to his delicate floss silk moustache, and he was contemplating a fresh appeal to his scented handkerchief and making the threatened bolt, as he termed it, with the cambric held to his nose, when Lady Littletown approached.

'Now, my dearest Richard,' she exclaimed, and her many years, the speck of gold near one top tooth, the wrinkles at the corners of her eyes, and the sugges-tions of untruthfulness about her hair, all seemed to be softened down and seen through an eyeglass tinted *à la rose*, 'I'm a very covetous person, and I always make a point, like the wicked old widow I am, of reserving the most *beau chevalier* for myself. Now you have to take me in, we two last; and you'll be obliged to help me out of my difficulties if there is anything to carve.'

Dick coloured a little with pride:

'And we, too, must have a pleasant chat about

mamma and the dear girls ; and, oh, I am so glad you took to the army and are quartered down here. It will be so pleasant for me; but I shall, for mamma's sake, watch all your doings. I am not going to have you turn out a *roué* like your wicked Major. Come along.'

So Dick took in her ladyship, feeling taller, and actually seeming to swell a little, as he found himself seated at his hostess's right hand. Then, the places being found, every guest's name neatly written on a porcelain *menu*, Lord Henry, at the foot of the table, closed his eyes, bent forward, and in a low, reverent voice said grace, to which Mr. Elbraham added a very audible ' Amen !' and the dinner commenced.

Of course it was all by way of paying her dues to society that things were done so well, for certainly the dinner was as exquisite as the table itself, with its decorations of plate and glass, amidst which, half hidden in almost a redundancy of exotic flowers, was a thoroughly choice dessert. Richard Millet, who rather trembled in the midst of his pride, and had twice in imagination seen wings of chicken, as he dis-membered a bird, flying in a cloud of brown sauce

into people's laps, was spared all trouble, for the
viands were served *à la Russe*, and were perfect of
their kind.

'I'm deuced glad I came,' thought Mr. Elbraham, as
the choice, well-iced wines reached him in turn, and
after several rather awkward attempts at conversation
with Clotilde he found himself getting on much
better.   For his companion, in spite of her delight at
being present at such a party, and having been affectionately kissed by Lady Littletown, and called 'My
dearest child,' was disappointed because Captain Glen
had not spoken to her, neither had he been chosen to
take her in to dinner.   But, then, he had looked at
her—looked at her several times.   He admired her.
There was no doubt about that.   His looks said so
plainly; and, for her part, there was something very
pleasant to her eyes in the well-built, manly fellow,
with his easy, indifferent ways and his gentlemanly,
chivalrous attention to her aunt ; who, poor soul ! was
nervous, and fluttered with the unusual excitement.

'I don't like him ; he's a dreadful creature,' said
Clotilde to herself, as her companion grew more at
home, and, after a glass or two of a very choice

champagne of unusual potency, began to talk to her
in a fashion somewhat suggestive of his style at
a private supper at the Rantan or at Latellier's,
and ladies who were in the habit of performing show
parts in public were present.

'I'm deuced glad I came. She's a devilish handsome girl, and I like her,' thought Mr. Elbraham, and
during his next remark, of course inadvertently, his
coat-sleeve touched Clotilde's firm, white, well-rounded
arm.

'And so you lead a very quiet, very retired life,'
said Lord Henry to Marie, as, scarcely partaking
of anything himself, he chivalrously devoted his
attention to his companion, enjoying her evident
delight and hearty young appetite, which as a rule
was none too well satisfied.

She, too, had been, in the midst of her delight
in her charming dress, the reflection of her handsome
self in Lady Littletown's mirror, that lady's affectionate
greeting, and the brilliant dinner-table, rather disappointed that she had not been taken in by Captain
Glen, or that dark handsome Major, or even by the
funny pretty little page style of officer; but by

degrees that wore off, and she listened with real pleasure to Lord Henry's words.

He was quite an elderly gentleman, but, then, he was a nobleman, with a truer feeling of admiration for the beautiful woman he had been called upon to escort. There was something delightfully new, too, in her ways. She was very different to the society young ladies he was accustomed to meet, all gush and strained style of conversation. Marie was as if fresh from a convent, and he was even amused with some of her naïve remarks.

The Honourable Misses Dymcox had given their nieces the most stringent instructions upon etiquette ; above all, they were not to taste wine ; but while Marie was answering a remark made by Lord Henry, one of the servants filled that faintly prismatic glass, like half a soap-bubble in its beauty, and from old habit Marie lifted the drinking vessel by her hand, tasted, found the clear sparkling wine delicious, and had sipped again and again.

The effect was trifling, but it did remove some of her diffidence, and she found herself chatting willingly enough to her cavalier.

'Oh yes ; a very, very retired life. We spend most of our time in the schoolroom, and when we take walks it is in the gardens or in the park with our aunts, at times when none of the London people are down.'

' Have you been on the Continent ?'

'Oh no,' replied Marie, 'not since Mr. Montaigne brought us over to the Palace ?'

' May I ask who is Mr. Montaigne ?'

' He was a very old friend of poor mamma's.'

' Poor mamma ?' said Lord Henry inquiringly.

'Oh yes ; poor mamma and papa died when we were very little girls, and we have been with our aunts ever since.'

Lord Henry sipped his wine, gazed sidewise at his beautiful companion, and sighed. He thought of Gertrude Millet, and let his eye rest from time to time upon her brother, vainly trying to trace a resemblance, and also that though Lady Millet had undoubtedly seemed pleased by his advances, Gertrude had been chilling, and Marie Dymcox was not.

Possibly, too, as the old man sighed, he thought that he had no time to lose now that he had been thinking that he would marry, and he sighed again as if in regret of something he had lost, something he might have had, but had been too careless or indifferent to win.

A close observer would have noticed that there were tears in his eyes just then. Lady Littletown was a close observer, and by the aid of her eyeglass she did notice it, and secretly hugged herself.

'But you go out a good deal—to parties, to concerts, or balls?'

'Oh no!' laughed Marie, and her white teeth showed beneath her coral lips, while Major Malpas, who was nearly opposite, looked at her intently from beneath his heavy eyelids, and softly stroked his moustache. 'I was never at a party before.'

'And do you like it?' said Lord Henry, beaming upon her, as, with a secret kind of satisfaction, he quietly admired the animated countenance beside him.

'Oh yes, yes,' she said softly. 'I can't help liking it very much.'

'Well,' said Lord Henry, smiling in quite a pleased manner, 'why should you help liking it?'

'I don't know,' she said thoughtfully; 'only we are

always so quiet at the Palace, and aunts have often said that too much gaiety was bad.'

'Too much, my dear child. Yes, certainly; but a little is very pleasurable, and innocent, and good.'

Marie's eyes, as they met his, said that they were delighted to hear it, and as she sat and let the quiet, chivalrous old gentleman draw her out, no one would have credited her with being one of the heroines of some of the school-room scenes in which poor little Ruth had been the victim.

Lord Henry Moorpark grew more and more thoughtful as he chatted on with his companion. There was something inexpressibly refreshing in Marie's words and ways, and he, too, congratulated himself upon the dinner-party, which he had looked upon as a nuisance, and to which he had come solely out of respect for Lady Littletown, turning out so pleasurable and fresh.

He was not the only elderly guest who thoroughly enjoyed the dinner, for the Honourable Isabella Dymcox partook of her share of the courses in a state of, for her, unwonted flutter. In accordance with the plotting and planning that had been at work in the Palace coterie, she had come fully prepared to give a furtive observation to what was going on with Clotilde and Marie, the children who, with her sister, she was fain to confess had arrived at a marriageable age; but from the moment she had laid her tremulous hand upon Marcus Glen's arm, and had been led by him to her seat, her nieces had been forgotten.

Certainly Glen had several times over exchanged glances with Clotilde, and taken notice of the fact that Elbraham was growing more and more familiar and loud; but all the same he had found ample time to devote himself with a good deal of assiduity to Miss Isabella, making her at first surprised and cold, soon after pleased and full of agreeable thoughts, and at last thoroughly gratified at the way in which her companion attended to her lightest wishes and conversed upon society at Hampton Court.

'I—I won't be so foolish as so think he means anything,' said Miss Isabella to herself; 'for he is quite young and manly-looking, almost handsome, while I am getting very old indeed, and all hope of *that* is past; but he is very nice and gentlemanly, and so very different to officers as a rule. I must say I like him very much.'

She showed, too, that she did as soon as the cold formal crust had been melted away, and Marcus was not slow to realize the fact.

He was perfectly honest, for he knew that the Honourable Isabella was the aunt of Clotilde, and being as impressionable as most young men of his age, he had felt to some extent the power of that lady's eyes. Under the circumstances, as he had been thrown with the relative, he had thought it fair campaigning to make friends with her, and this he had done to such an extent that the attentions she had received, and a glass or two of wine, made the lady very communicative, and far happier than her sister, who found the dinner much less to her taste.

For Major Malpas was not best pleased at having to take her in, and he had confined himself to the most frigid civilities. He was perfectly gentlemanly, but as the dinner wore on he grew more polite, and by consequence the Honourable Philippa became icy in her manner, till at last she seemed to be frozen stiff.

'Humph!' he thought, 'better have gone and sat with Renée Morrison. Yes,' he continued, staring hard at Dick, 'your sister, my half-fledged cockerel.

The other guests merely formed chorus to the principal singers in the little social opera, but they were wonderfully led by Lady Littletown, whose tongue formed her conductor's baton, by which she swayed them with a practised ease.

She had a word in season for everyone where it was needful to keep up the balance of the parts, and wonderfully skilful was her way. She gave a great deal of her time to everybody, but little Richard Millet never missed any of her attentions. In a very short time she had quite won his confidence, and knew that Major Malpas was a regular plunger, that Captain Glen was the dearest and best fellow in the world, that he hadn't any more vice in him than a child, that they were the dearest of friends, and that Marcus had only about two hundred and fifty a year besides his pay.

'I begin to like Hampton Court, Lady Littletown,' said the boy warmly, for the champagne had been frequent.

'I'm sure you'll love the place when you begin to know us better. Of course you will come to all my "at homes?"'

'That I will,' exclaimed the delighted youth. 'By the way, Lady Littletown, what lovely girls those Miss Dymcoxes are!'

'Yes, are they not?' replied Lady Littletown; 'but oh, fie, fie, fie! This will not do. I will not listen to a single word. I'm not going to lend myself to any match-making. What would Lady Millet say?'

'But, really, Lady Littletown——'

'Oh dear me, no; I will not listen. I know too well, sir, what you officers are—so wicked and reckless, and given to breaking ladies' hearts. I think I shall absolutely forbid you even approaching them when you come up to the drawing-room. I would not for the world be the means of causing any heart diseases amongst my guests.'

'But surely, Lady Littletown, a fellow may admire at a distance?'

'Oh dear no,' said her ladyship playfully; 'I think not. I'm afraid you are a very bad, dangerous man, and I shall have to withdraw my invitation.'

Dick Millet pleaded; the invitation was not withdrawn; and the little fellow was better satisfied with himself than he had felt for months.

'It's an uncommonly well got-up affair, after all,' he thought; 'but I wish the ladies would go now. I want to get the wine over, and go up to the drawing-room.'

To the little fellow's satisfaction the long-drawn-out repast did come to an end, that cleverly-managed signal was given which acts electrically at a certain stage of a dinner; the ladies rose, and in place of one of the younger gentlemen opening the door, Lord Henry performed that duty, a genial but half-sad smile playing about his thin, closely-shaven lips, as Marie looked up in his face in passing. Then the last lady went out, and the gentlemen closed up to their coffee and wine.

Somehow or other, Marcus Glen found himself now near Lord Henry, and while a knot of listeners heard Mr. Elbraham's opinion upon the Eastern Question, especially with regard to the new Sultan and the position of Egypt, the young officer entered into a quiet discussion upon the history of the old Palace, and was surprised and pleased to find how much his companion knew of the past days of the old red-brick building, but above all at the genial, winning manner the old gentleman possessed.

Acting the part of host now for the time being, he soon proposed that they should adjourn, for there was a strange longing within him to be within sight and hearing of Marie.

'Ah, to be sure,' said Elbraham; 'if I wanted to invest, gentlemen, I should say Egyptian bonds. By all means, let's join the ladies.'

He, too, had come to the conclusion that he should like 'another talk to that girl.' But the drawing-room was filling fast, and there were no more *tête-à-têtes.* Arthur Litton arrived soon after ten, and his chief approached him to shake hands, as if they had not met for some time.

'Well?' said Litton.

'Stunning, sir, stunning! 'Bove par.'

'Oh!'

'Deuced good dinner, Litton, 'pon my soul. People not half so snobbish as I expected to find them. I say, look here. What do you think of that piece of goods?'

He indicated Clotilde, about whom Dick Millet was now hovering; but who had turned from him to listen to a remark just made by Glen.

'Hum, ha!' said Litton critically. 'Oh, that's one of the Dymcox girls, isn't it?'

'I didn't ask you anything about who she is; I said what do you think of her?'

'Not bad-looking, I should say,' replied Litton coolly; 'but nothing particular.'

'Oh, you be blowed!' said the great financier, and he screwed his short thick neck down a little lower into his chest, and turned away.

'Well, Lady Littletown, how do matters make themselves?' said Litton quietly, when, after a time, her ladyship passed his way.

'Oh, *Arturo, mio caro*,' said her ladyship, tickling the centre stud in his shirt-front with the end of her closed fan. '*Maravigliosamente.* My dear boy, it is wonderful. You shall have a rich wife, Arthur, if you are good, and this affair is *un fait accompli.*'

'Why didn't you try a bit of German, too?' muttered Litton, as her ladyship passed on. 'Here, I must get on with some of these officers; perhaps they'd take me to their quarters, and give me a smoke and an S. and B. Hang this tea! I forgot, though, I promised Potiphar to go home with him. Hang the beast! but it will save me a fare.'

Everyone was delighted. Lady Littletown was charmed over and over again, but when at last an obsequious footman, who seemed to be shod with velvet, whispered to the Honourable Philippa that her carriage had arrived, that lady, who felt very tired and sleepy, said mentally, 'Thank goodness!'

But it was half an hour later before she made a move, and the drawing-rooms were growing unbearably hot with the chattering, buzzing crowd.

Suddenly there was silence, as the Honourable Misses Dynicox rose to go.

Lady Littletown was so sorry the evening had been so short, but she managed to exchange meaning looks.

'I think, yes,' she whispered; and the Honourable Philippa nodded and tightened her lips.

'Good-night, my sweet darling,' said Lady Little-town, kissing Clotilde affectionately. 'Mind you come and see me soon. Good-night, dearest Marie. How well you look to-night, child!'

Then her ladyship saw through her square eye-glass, with the broad chased gold rim, Elbraham, podgy, stout and puffy, take Clotilde down to the carriage, followed by Lord Henry with Marie, and Captain Glen with the Honourable Isabella, and little Richard Millet with the Honourable Philippa; every-one but Joseph being perfectly ignorant of the fact that Mr. Buddy had been imbibing largely of the stimulants plentifully handed round to the various servants outside.

But the ladies were duly packed inside, the jangling door was banged to, and Joseph, having mounted to the box beside Mr. Buddy, perhaps only out of regard for his own safety, assumed the reins of government himself, and steered the fly to the Palace doors.

'Good-night, children,' said the Honourable Misses Dymcox in duet. 'Take care of your dresses what-ever you do!'

'Oh, Rie!' cried Clotilde, as soon as they were in their bedroom.

'Oh, Clo!' cried Marie. Then, crossing to the farther door to the cupboard in which Ruth's bed was squeezed—' 'Sleep, Ruthy?'

'No, Marie,' was the reply, as a troubled, pale face was lifted from the pillow.

'Why, I declare she has been crying!' said Clotilde. 'There, jump up and help us to undress, Cindy, and we'll tell you all about the prince and the ball. You weren't there, were you?'

No; Cinderella, otherwise Ruth Allerton, had not been there; but she had been crying bitterly, for she had had a fright.

CHAPTER XI.

FAMILY MATTERS.

CAPTAIN ROBERT MILLET'S lunch was carried up to him upon a very stiff, narrow tray, which took dishes and plates one after the other in a long row. It was evidently something or several somethings very savoury and nice from the odours exhaled, but everything was carefully covered over.

It was no easy task, the carriage of that long, narrow tray from the basement to the back drawing-room on the first floor, especially as there were gravies and other liquids on the tray; but Valentine Vidler and his wife had taken up breakfasts, lunches, and dinners too many thousand times to be in any difficulty now.

So, starting from the dark kitchen, where coppers,

pewters, and tins shone like so many moons amidst
the gloom, the odd couple each took an end of the
tray, which was quite six feet long, and Vidler's own
invention. Salome went first, backwards, and Vidler
followed over the level, when, as the little woman
reached the mat at the foot of the kitchen stairs, there
was a pause, while she held the tray with one hand
and gave her long garments a hitch, so as to hold one
end in her teeth and not tread upon them as she went
up backwards. Then, stooping and holding the tray
as low as she could, she began to ascend, Vidler
following and gradually raising his end to preserve
the level of the tray till he held it right above his
head.

This raising and lowering in ascent and upon level
was all carried out in the most exact and regular
way—in fact, so practised had the old couple grown
in the course of years, that they could have carried a
brimming glass of water up the gloomy stairs without spilling a drop. Hence, then, they reached the
drawing-room with the tray preserving its equilibrium
from bottom to top.

As soon as they were inside Salome placed her end

upon the little bracket while Vidler retained his;
then she went out of the room, took up a big, soft
drumstick, and gave three gentle taps on a gong that
hung in its frame—three taps at long intervals, which
sounded like the boomings of a bell at the funeral of
a fish and a fowl—and then returned to the drawing-
room and stood on the right-hand side of the panel
close to the wall with one hand raised.

As she took her place the panel was softly slid back
towards her. Then she took off the first cover, Vidler
acting in conjunction, made the long tray glide slowly
forwards into the opening, its end evidently resting
on something within. Then two hands appeared, a
knife and fork were used, with a glass at intervals,
and the fish was discussed.

As soon as the knife and fork were laid down
Salome whipped off two more covers, and the tray
glided in a couple of feet further, both the lady and
her lord keeping their eyes fixed upon the floor.

The calmness and ease with which all this was
carried on indicated long practice, and for precision
no amount of drilling could have secured greater
regularity. As the knife and fork fell upon the plate

again there was a pause, for a pint decanter and glass were pushed opposite the thin white hands that now approached, and, removing the stopper, filled the glass. Then a cover was raised, and the tray glided onward once more, with some steaming asparagus on toast; and after a short pause the cold, colourless voice was heard to repeat a short grace, the tray was slowly withdrawn, the panel glided to, and Vidler and his little wife bore the remains of the luncheon to the lower regions.

Hardly had the tray been set down before there was a double knock, and on going upstairs Vidler found John Huish at the front door.

'Would Captain Millet give me an interview, Vidler?' he asked.

The little man looked at him sidewise, then tried the other eye, and ended by standing out of the way and letting the visitor enter, shutting out the light again as carefully as before.

'I'll try, sir,' he said; 'I don't think he will. I was just going to take up that,' he continued, pointing to a basket of coloured scraps of print. 'He's about to begin a new counterpane to-day.'

' A new what ?' said Huish.

' A new counterpane for the Home Charity.
That'll be six he has made this year. I'll show you
the last.'

He led Huish into the darkened dining-room, and
showed him a wonderfully neat piece of needlework,
a regular set pattern, composed of hundreds upon
hundreds of tiny scraps of cotton print.

' Makes 'em better than many women could, and
almost in the dark,' said the little man ; ' but I'll go
up and see. Miss Millet and her sister have not
been gone long.'

' What !' cried Huish, ' from here ?''

' Gone nearly or quite an hour ago, sir. Been a
good deal lately.'

' My usual fortune,' muttered Huish excitedly.
' But go up,' he said aloud ; ' I particularly want to
have a few words with him.'

' I don't think it's of any use, sir ; but I'll see,'
repeated the little man ; and he went upstairs, to
return at the end of about five minutes to beckon the
visitor up, and left him facing the panel.

It was evident that the young man had been there

before, as he took a seat, and waited patiently for the
panel to unclose, which it did at last, but not until
quite a quarter of an hour had passed.

' Well, John Huish,' said the voice, ' what do you
want ?'

It was rather a chilling reception for one who had
come upon such a mission ; but he was prepared for
it, and dashed at once into the object of his visit, in
spite of the peculiarity of having to address himself
to a square opening in the wall.

' I have come for advice and counsel,' said Huish
firmly.

' You, a man of the world, living in the world, come
to such an anchorite as I !' said the voice—' as I, who
have for pretty well thirty years been dead to society
and its ways ?'

' Yes,' said Huish. ' I come to you because you
can help.'

' How much do you want, John Huish ?' said the
voice. ' Give me the pen and ink.'

The thin white hand appeared impatiently at the
opening, with the fingers clutching as if to take the
pen.

'No, no, no!' said the young man hastily. 'It is not that. Let me tell you,' he exclaimed, as the fingers ceased to clutch impatiently at the air and the white hand rested calmly upon the edge of the opening—'let me speak plainly, for I am not ashamed of it—I am in love.'

There was a faint sigh here, hardly audible to the young man, who went on :

'I come to you for help and advice.'

'What can I do to help ? As for advice,' said the voice coldly, 'I will do what I can. Is she worthy of your love ?'

'Worthy?' cried Huish, flushing. 'She is an angel.'

'Yes,' said the voice, with a sigh. 'They all are. But, tell me, does she refuse you.'

'No, sir.'

'Then what more do you want ? Who and what is she ?'

These last words were said with more approach to interest, and the fingers began to tap the edge of the opening.

'It is presumption on my part,' said Huish, growing

excited, and rising to stride up and down the room, 'for I am poor and unworthy of her.'

'No true honourable man is unworthy of the woman he loves,' said the voice calmly, 'though he may, perhaps, be unsuited. Go on. Who is the lady?'

'Who is she, sir? I believed that you must know. It is your niece—Gertrude.'

'My God!'

It was almost a whisper, but John Huish heard it, and saw that the thin white hand seemed to be jerked upwards, falling slowly back, though, to remain upon the edge of the opening trembling.

'I shock you, sir, by my announcement,' said Huish bitterly.

'No—yes—no; not shock—surprise me greatly.' There was a pause, and the fingers trembled as they were now and again raised, then grew steady as they were laid down. 'But tell me,' it continued, trembling and becoming less cold, 'does Gertrude return your love?'

'Oh yes, Heaven bless her, yes!' cried the young man fervently; and there was another silence, such as might have ensued had the owner of the voice been trying to master some emotion.

'What more, then, do you want?' said the voice, now greatly changed. 'You, an honourable young man, in love with a girl who is all sweetness and purity. It is strange; but it is the will of God. Marry her, and may He bless the union!'

'Captain Millet, you make me very, very happy,' cried the young man; and before the hand could be removed it was seized and pressed in his strong grasp.

It was withdrawn directly, and a fresh silence ensued, when the voice said softly:

'And my brother, does he approve?'

'Oh yes; I think so,' replied Huish; 'but——'

'The mother objects—of course. She has made her choice. Who is it?'

'Lord Henry Moorpark.'

'A man nearly three times her age. It would be a crime. You will not permit such an outrage against her youth. Moorpark must be mad.'

'What can I do, sir?' cried Huish. 'That is why I ask your help and counsel.'

' Bah!' said the voice contemptuously. ' You are young and strong ; you have your wits ; Gertrude loves you, and you ask me for help and counsel! John Huish, at your age, under such circumstances, it would have been a bold man who would have robbed me of my prize. There, go—go, young man, and think and act. Poor Gertrude! she has a mother who makes Mammon her God—a woman who has broken one of her children's hearts ; do not let her break that of the other. Go now, I am weary : this has been a tiring day. You can come to me again.'

' Do not let her break that of the other,' said John Huish to himself as the panel slowly closed ; and from that moment the dim twilight of the shuttered house became to him glorious with light, and he went away feeling joyous and elastic as he had not felt for days. As he neared his chambers a thin, gray, hard-faced-looking woman, who had stood watching for quite an hour, stepped out of a doorway and touched him on the arm.

He turned sharply, and she said in a low voice :

' I must see you. Come to-morrow night at the old time.'

Before he could speak she had hurried away, turned down the next street, and was gone.

'To-morrow night—the old time?' said Huish, gazing after her, and then raising his hat to place his hand upon his forehead. 'Quite cool. Is it fancy? Why should that woman speak to me?'

Then, turning upon his heel, he entered the door of his chambers, and set himself to work to think over his interview, and to devise some plan for defeating Lady Millet in her projected enter- prise.

'It would shock her,' he said at last; 'but when she knows of her uncle's views she might be influenced. She must, she shall be. The poor old man's words have given me strength, and I shall win, after all. But what slaves we are to custom and prejudice! I ought not to be the man to study them in such a case as this.'

Then the words just spoken to him at the door came back to puzzle and set him thinking of several other encounters—or fancied encounters with people whom he felt that he had never seen before.

'I don't know what to say to it,' he thought;

'Stonor ought to know; but somehow I feel as if he had not grasped my case. There, I will not trouble about that now.'

He kept the thoughts which troubled him from his brain for a time, but they soon forced themselves back with others.

' I wonder,' he mused, ' what took place in the past? There must have been something. My father and mother must have known Captain Millet very intimately. He received his injury from some fall, and Dr. Stonor saved his limb, I believe. But there's a reticence about all that time which is aggravating. I suppose I must wait, and when I learn everything which puzzles me now, it will be only shadowy and vague. Only my mother always asks about the Captain with so tender a tone of respect. Ah, well! I must wait.'

At about the same time that John Huish was pondering over his state in connection with his love affairs, Renée Morrison called in her carriage for her sister, bore her off to where she thought they could be alone, and sent the carriage back. The place chosen was the Park, which, though pretty well thronged with people, seemed to them solitary, as they strolled across toward the Row.

Gertrude was very silent, for she felt that Renée had something important to say ; but the minutes sped on, and their scattered remarks had been of the most commonplace character, and at last, as she glanced sideways, Gertrude saw that if her sister were to confide her troubles and be the recipient of those effervescing in her own breast she herself must speak.

'You do not confide in me, Renée dear,' she said tenderly, as they took a couple of chairs beneath one of the spreading trees. 'Why do you not always make me more your confidant ? One feels as if one could talk out here in the park, where there are no walls to listen. Come, dear, why do you not tell me all ?'

' Because I feel that my husband's secrets are in my keeping, and that I should be doing wrong to speak of what he does.'

' Not wrong in confiding in me, Renée. You are not happy. Oh, Ren, Ren, why did you consent ? Trouble, and so soon !'

'Don't talk to me like that, now, Gerty,' cried Renée in a low, passionate voice, 'because it was mamma's will that we should marry well and have establishments, and satisfy her pride. Sometimes I think it would have been better if I had never been born.'

'Oh, Ren, Ren,' her sister whispered, pressing her hand. 'But Frank—he is kind to you?'

'Yes,' said Renée sadly; 'he is never angry with me.'

'But I mean kind and loving and attentive, as your husband should be?' said Gertrude softly.

Renée looked at her with a sad, heavy look, and now that the first confidence had been made, her heart was open to her sister.

'Gertrude,' she whispered to her, 'he never loved me!'

'Oh, Ren dear, think what you are saying!'

'I do think, dear, and I say it once more. He never loved me.'

'But, Renée, you have been kind and loving to him.'

'Yes, as tender as a woman could be to the man

she had sworn to love ; but he does not care for me, and I am haunted.'

'Haunted, Renée !'

'Yes ; hush ! Here is Major Malpas.'

Gertrude glanced in the direction taken by her sister's eyes, and her heart seemed to be compressed as by a cold hand, as she turned indignantly to her sister.

'Renée !' she said, in a horrified whisper, 'oh, do not say you care for him still !'

'Gertrude !' cried Renée, catching her hand, 'how dare you say that ! I hate—I detest him ! I thought him a gentleman once, and I did love him ; but that was over when I married Frank, and since then he has haunted me ; he follows me everywhere, and Frank makes him his constant companion, and he leads him away.'

'Oh, this is dreadful !'

'Dreadful !' cried Renée, 'I feel at times that I cannot bear it. Come away : he has seen us, and is coming here.'

'Is—is that Mr. Huish ?' whispered Gertrude, gazing in another direction.

' Yes. Who is the dark lady on his arm ?'

' I do not know,' said Gertrude quietly. 'Some friend, perhaps ; but, look, is not that Frank ?'

She drew her sister's attention towards a phaeton in which Frank Morrison was driving a handsome-looking woman dressed in the height of fashion ; and directly Renée saw him plainly the Major came up.

'What a delightful meeting, Miss Millet !' he said. 'Mrs. Morrison, I hope I shall not be *de trop ?*'

'My husband's friends have too great a claim on me,' said Renée quietly, as she left her seat and moved in the direction of her own home ; but she kept glancing in the direction taken by the phaeton.

It was cleverly managed, and as if Malpas knew exactly when the carriage would next come by, timing his place so well that the sisters were close to the railings as the dashing pair scattered some of the earth over the young wife's dress.

' Who is that with Frank Morrison, Major Malpas ?' said Gertrude quickly.

' I beg your pardon ?' he said.

'That fashionably-dressed lady in my brother-in-law's phaeton. There they go.'

'Indeed!' said the Major. 'I was not looking. Are you sure it was he?'

'Certain,' replied Gertrude.

'My dear Mrs. Morrison, is anything the matter?' cried the Major, with a voice full of sympathy.

'No, nothing,' said the young wife, who was now deadly pale. 'May I ask you—to leave us?'

'Yes,' he said earnestly; 'but I shall not go. Pray take my arm. Miss Millet, your sister is ill. I fear you have been imprudent and have taxed her strength. I must see her safely home, or I could not face Morrison again.'

'He haunts me!' thought Gertrude to herself, as she recalled her sister's words, and found that the Major persisted in walking by her side till they reached Chesham Place, where, murmuring his satisfaction that Renée seemed better, he left the sisters in the hall.

'All things come to the man who waits,' he muttered to himself, as he went off smiling.

'Renée,' said Gertrude, as soon as they were alone,

'have you ever encouraged him in any way since your marriage? How is it he seems to have such a hold upon you?'

'I do not know—I cannot tell,' said Renée wearily, as, with brow contracted, she sat thinking of the scene in the Park. 'But do not mention him—do not think of him, Gertrude dear; he is as nothing in face of this new misery.'

'New misery?' said Gertrude innocently.

'Yes,' cried Renée passionately; 'do you not see? Oh, Frank, Frank!' she moaned, 'why do you treat me so?'

Gertrude, upon whom all this came like a revelation, strove to comfort her, and to point out that her fears might be mere exaggerations, but her sister turned sharply.

'You do not understand these things, Gertrude,' she said. 'He does not love me as he should, and, knowing this, Major Malpas has never ceased to try and tempt him away from me—to the clubs—to gambling parties, from which he comes home hot and feverish; and now it seems that worse is to follow. Oh, mother, mother! you have secured me an establishment which I would gladly change for the humblest cottage, if it contained my husband's faithful love.'

Gertrude's heart beat fast at these words, and a falteri ~ purpose became strengthened.

'But, Ren darling,' she whispered; 'have you spoken to him and tried to win him from such associations? Frank is so good at heart.'

'Yes,' sighed Renée; 'but so weak and easily led away. Spoken to him, Gertrude? No, dear. As his wife, I have felt that I must ignore such things. I would not know that he visited such places—that he gambled—that he returned home excited. I have put all such thoughts aside, and met him always with the same smile of welcome, when my heart has been well-nigh broken.'

'My poor sister!' whispered Gertrude, drawing her head to her breast and thinking of the husband and establishment that her mother had arranged for her to possess.

'But this I feel that I cannot bear,' cried Renée impetuously. 'It is too great an outrage!'

'Oh, Ren, Ren!' whispered Gertrude, 'do not judge

him too rashly ; wait and see—it may be all a mistake.'

'Mistake!' said Renée bitterly ; 'did you not see him driving that woman out ? Did you not see her occupying the place that should be mine?'

'Yes—yes,' faltered Gertrude ; 'but still there may be some explanation.'

'Yes,' said Renée at last, as she dried her tears and sat up, looking very cold and stern ; 'there may be, and we will wait and see. At all events, I will not say one single harsh word.'

Gertrude left her at last quite calm and composed, the brougham being ordered for her use, and she sat back thinking of John Huish with the dark lady ; but only to smile, for no jealous fancy troubled her breast.

END OF VOL. I.

BILLING AND SONS, PRINTERS, GUILDFORD.

www.ingramcontent.com/pod-product-compliance
Lightning Source LLC
Chambersburg PA
CBHW031426020726
47499CB00005B/1609